The
Mob Zone

JOSEPH DeMATTEO

HIGH DUNES PRESS

Printed in the United States of America

ISBN 978-1-7360147-0-7 (paperback)

ISBN 978-1-7360147-1-4 (ebook)

Book design by TeaBerryCreative.com

Contents

Introduction

You are traveling through another dimension, a dimension of crime, not punishment, murder, but not manslaughter; a dimension where vice is nice. A place where time is something you do—but only when you can't bribe a juror. You're moving into a land that lacks both morality and legality. A land of wrong, not right. A world…where only rats survive.

You've just crossed over into the MOB ZONE.

Benny and Nicky Go for a Ride

The burgundy Coupe de Ville slowed as it pulled alongside the curb. Mirror image row houses, sided with brittle asphalt shingles, lined the dark South Philadelphia street. To an outsider, they all looked the same. Nicky "The Knife" Nunzio knew exactly which one to stop at.

As the car's headlights lit up the pavement, Benny "Big Foot" Bennato stepped outside. His flowing white hair shimmered as brightly as a supermoon in the pre-dawn darkness.

It was an unusually cool May morning. Carrying a small bag, Benny descended the short stairway one step at a time until he reached the sidewalk. Convinced there was no frost, with his free hand, he reached for the Cadillac's door handle.

"Jesus, man. Fuckin' freezin' out." Benny's large frame fell onto the tufted leather seat. He tossed the bag in back.

Known for his impeccable sense of style, the short fat man wore a dark suit, crisp white shirt and bright red tie. Nicky smelled the cologne—*Polo*, in the green bottle.

"Mornin' Benny. Here, turn up the heat." Nicky slid the temperature control lever into the red. Wearing a black leather blazer, Nicky knew he might be warm, but deferred to his elder passenger.

"Ah, that's more like it. Reminds me of delivering pizza as a kid. I'd put the boxes on the floor and turn up the heat. Even in the summer."

Nicky laughed.

Benny raised his hands to the vents and rubbed them together vigorously. "Would keep the pies warm. Then I'd drive like a crazy man to keep 'em from gettin' cold. Got a better tip."

Nicky drove off. "Now days they deliver pizza in those thermal bags. Cook it under red tubes. Probably give you a disease."

"*Apizza*," Benny barked. "That's how you know it's good. Never eat where the sign says pizza. Like in New Haven, the signs say *apizza*. They don't fuck around up there."

"New Haven, huh? You spent time in New Haven?"

"I'm an old fuck. I spent time in lotsa places."

"Oh, yeah? What kinda places?"

"Places. The wife likes Florida. Her sister lives in Pompano Beach. Drove down a couple times. I put my feet in the water. Can't swim. Even if I could, that ain't my thing—sharks."

"Florida's nice."

Benny waved his hand forward dismissively. "*PFFT,* not for me. Too hot. Get a rash between my legs. How 'bout you? Travel much?"

Nicky shrugged. "Head up to New York every now and then. Atlantic City. Usual whorin' 'round shit."

"Like to party, eh? I can tell. Good lookin' guy like you. Why the hell not? Only live once. Fat fuck like me, at my age, I'd rather stay home and eat."

"I bet you had your share a broads in your day."

Benny sat up straight and puffed out his chest. "Did awright. But c'mon? Probably not like you. Tall, handsome, no belly. Bet ya ain't even got no back hair."

"Sister's a hairdresser. Tears it right out."

Benny winced. "Fuck that shit. Wife just scratches it when it gets itchy."

Benny and Nicky were members of the same family but belonged to different crews. Benny worked for Sal "The Snake" Magnoli, while Nicky took orders from Virgille "The Virgin" Volpe. Everyone answered to

"Easy" Eddie Iacobelli, the "Don" of South Philly.

The two capos had never worked together before and only knew each other casually. Benny was an old timer, reliable and loyal to the end. Nicky was younger and a bit of a loose cannon; that's why Eddie liked him. Given his talent for cutting, he was also what was known as a *Specialist*. Brought in for specific jobs. A shared resource, so to speak. While Eddie was fond of the knife-wielding playboy, he only entrusted him on high profile assignments with the supervision of a veteran. Not that he would turn rat, but with a reputation as a hothead, he might trip up on account of unchecked emotions and create a mess. A mess that required cleaning. Cleaning and unwanted attention that Eddie wanted no part of. Benny knew how to get a job done—he got in and out, quick and quiet.

Eddie, was a maverick among mob bosses—his peers considered him ruthless, the press called him a sociopath and his enemies feared him more than death itself. Law enforcement deemed him untouchable and long gave up ever trying to put him away. Unlike traditional heads of families, the *Don* of South Philly played by a different set of rules. He had earned a well-deserved reputation for operating outside the traditional boundaries of organized crime. When he ordered a hit, the result went beyond a typical mob rubout: gruesome, barbaric and totally unexpected.

While some godfathers might seek a reasonable solution to a problem—a negotiated settlement or perhaps a win-win—Eddie's M.O. was to go off half-cocked and wreak as much havoc as possible. Drawing inspiration from Hollywood, he once had an adversary buried alive inside the slaughtered carcass of the victim's prized thoroughbred underneath the finish line of the Philadelphia Park racetrack. Understandably, his soldiers were always on edge.

Nicky turned onto the entrance ramp of I95 and headed north. He adjusted the rearview mirror so he could see the back seat. "What ya got in the bag? Thought we weren't stayin' over."

"We ain't. Just some things we need."

"What kinda things?"

"Things. The kind we need."

"Gonna be a long ride. Don't know why we had to drive."

"Don't fly. Planes crash."

"Cars crash too."

"Not like planes. Maybe a fender bender, but at least you don't fall outta the sky."

Nicky shrugged.

"Pay attention. Imagine sittin' in a bus and someone hoistin' it 40,000 feet into the air." Benny made a sour face and shook his head. "Not for me."

"Still, gonna be a long ride. You been to Boston before?"

"What'd I say? I been to lotsa places. That's why Eddie wanted me to handle this thing. I know Boston. Can get in and out. Quick and quiet."

"Eddie ask you to take me?"

"Eddie don't ask no one nuttin'. He *told* me to take you. Need a knife for this job. No noise. In and out. Quick and quiet."

Nicky pursed his lips and nodded.

The sun rose as they crossed the Jersey state line.

"Get a good night's rest?" Nicky asked.

"Slept like a baby. Doctor put me on a snorin' machine. Keeps me breathin'."

"Keeps you breathin'?"

Benny squeezed his double chin. "Too fat. Doc told me to lose weight." He waved his hand dismissively. "'Yeah right,' I said. At my age? Wife couldn't take it. Said my snorin' shook the house. Used to wake her up."

"So he gave you a machine?"

"Yeah. No, first I had to make a movie. They hook ya up to a buncha wires like Frankenstein and watch ya while ya sleepin'."

Nicky grimaced. "Sounds like they sent ya to the chair."

"God forbid." Benny made the sign of the cross. "Yeah, at first I thought it was little weird. I mean, they film you sleepin' all night, right there in your boxers. Who knows where those tapes end up." Benny tapped his index fingers on the dashboard like he was typing. "Next thing you know, some Oriental guy on the other side a the world is watchin' ya on the *compooder* playin' with himself."

Nicky raised his eyebrows.

"I don't know. All I know is, now I sleep like a baby."

"Can't argue with that."

Benny raised his right hand. "God strike me dead. I'm not makin' it up. You oughta get one. Only thing wakes my wife up now is when I make a bomb."

Nicky pursed his lips and nodded. He prayed he made it back to Philly without experiencing the combination of Benny's gaseous fumes mixed with the green *Polo*.

"How old you now?" Benny asked.

"Forty-two this August."

Benny stared in wide-eyed amazement. "You paint your hair. Don't tell me you don't. You paint it, don't ya?"

Nicky shook his head. "Nah, no need. Got no gray."

"You don't paint your hair? I'd swear you paint it."

"Why you ask? Your wife try and get ya to paint yours?"

"You shittin' me?" Benny patted his silver mane. "Says it makes me look like a movie star. Rake it real nice every mornin'."

"And that ain't no wig?"

"Fuck, no. Wouldn't be caught dead wearin' a rug."

"There you go."

"How 'bout your old lady? You think she'd like it if you end up all white like me?"

"Won't have to worry 'bout it. Threw the tub a shit out. Had enough. Divorce bankrupted me, but it was worth it."

"Sorry to hear that. I didn't know."

"No worries. For the best. Bitch crucified me for twenty fuckin' years. Said all I cared 'bout was chasin' broads."

"You slap her around?"

Nicky shook his head. "Don't believe in that shit. With women that is."

Benny shrugged. "Sometimes ya gotta do what ya gotta do. Got no choice. Kids?"

"Nah. She never stopped takin' the pill. Said I'd make a horrible father. Told her she shoulda knew mine."

"That's good. Harder with kids."

Nicky chose not to respond. He slipped on his aviators and glanced at the driver's side mirror.

Benny flipped his visor down. "Don't get me wrong, love my daughter. But kids are tough. Always cleanin' up after 'em. Even when they get older. Ask anybody. Me, I hadda rough up my son-in-law a few times. Lazy bastard. Never ends."

"What kinda job makes it so we gotta be quiet?"

Benny shifted in his seat. He nudged the temperature

lever toward the blue. "Sun's heatin' up the car. Don't wanna sweat."

Nicky cringed—Benny's pit juice mixed with the green *Polo*. "Crack the window. Get some fresh air."

"Too loud. Can't talk."

"So, what about the job? Why we gotta be quiet? Don't have permission to work in Boston?"

"Eddie don't need no permission. Gotta be a quiet job, that's all. Quick too. Just listen to me and everythin'll be fine." Benny's stubby finger stabbed at the window switch. A rush of loud air whipped through the car.

Nicky recalled the two reasons Benny earned the name, "Big Foot". The first was, before he whacked a guy, he would shoot him in the foot. The other was, Benny had wide flat feet.

Nicky nodded toward the passenger's side floor. "How the dogs doin'? Still wearin' those monster shoes? Ya know, the ones ya had to stand in cement to make?"

"Yes and no. 'Pends on the day. My daughter made me stop wearin' 'em 'round the house. Used to scare the grandkids. Said I looked like *Herman Munster*. These slippers work pretty good." He raised his foot. "They call 'em *moccasins*. Like Indians wear. Only black leather, not that brown suede shit. *Ferragamo*. Soft. Feels like I'm walkin' barefoot."

"Expensive?"

"Buddy a mine sells 'em outta his trunk."

"Speakin' a Injuns, how 'bout we stop at those casinos? Take a break. Do some gamblin'. Grab some chow. Win a few bucks. Fuck some whores. Like I said, gonna be a long ride."

Benny shook his head. "Gotta get up and back today. In and out. Quick and quiet. Don't need no whores. We'll eat in Boston. I know a few places. Been there before."

Nicky nodded. "Gotta piss. Don't think I can make it to Vince Lombardi. Woodrow Wilson's up ahead."

"They got a Roy Rogers there? Could go for a Trigger Burger."

"Too early, no?"

"Yeah, maybe you're right. I'll just stretch my feet."

"Might as well. Like I said, gonna be a long ride."

Benny frowned.

Nicky pulled into the rest area, parked and headed for the men's room. Emerging a minute later, he spotted Benny in the gift shop chatting with the young woman at the cash register.

Benny motioned toward a display table a few feet away. "How those Jersey T-shirts sellin'?"

"Not so good," she said.

Benny pursed his lips, raised his eyebrows and nodded.

. . .

Six hours later, the dated land yacht passed under the Prudential Center, entered the O'Neill Tunnel and turned off the exit for the North End.

"Starvin'," Nicky said.

"Don't worry," Benny said. "That's why we're goin' here first. Too early for the job. I know a few places. Been here before."

Nicky turned onto Hanover Street and parked. "Smells good," he said, stepping out of the car. Anything smelled better than the green *Polo*.

"That's how you know it's no good." Benny rolled onto the sidewalk and adjusted his jacket and tie. "Tourist trick. They pump ga'lic air outta vents. Buy it in cans."

Nicky pursed his lips and nodded.

"C'mon. Follow me. I know a few places. Been here before."

"What about the bag?"

"What about it?"

"It gonna be okay in the car?"

"Don't worry 'bout it. Nuttin' worth nuttin'. Besides, look around. You think anyone's gonna break into a Coupe de Ville in this neighborhood?"

Nicky pursed his lips and nodded.

After passing half a dozen restaurants, they stopped in front of a small trattoria.

"How 'bout this one?" Nicky asked. "It don't smell."

Benny peered through the window. "Not sure if I been here before. What the fuck, let's try it. I'm starvin'."

A curtain separated the dining area from the cramped vestibule. Sawdust dotted the white tiled floor. Colorful prints of the Italian countryside hung on the yellow stucco walls. Nicky assumed it was a beer and wine only kind of place since there was no sign of a bar.

"Looks classy," Benny said.

"You think? Those paintings look kinda cheap. Shouldn't they have photos a celebrities with the owner?"

"Nah. That's how you know it's a tourist trap." He nodded toward several male waiters. "Plus, no broads waitin' tables. That's a good sign."

While only two other parties were dining, the rustic eatery appeared to be able to accommodate perhaps fifty patrons. A family occupied a booth toward the back and a young couple sat at a linen covered table in the center of the room. Benny chose a spot by the window.

A middle-aged balding man, wearing a black waist apron, approached with two large leather folders.

Benny waved his hands from side to side. "No menus." He leaned forward and lowered his voice. "I'll do the orderin'."

Nicky pursed his lips and nodded.

"What's good today?" Benny asked.

"Everything is good, *Signore*."

"Tell me. Now be honest. Is the pasta pre-cooked? Because if it's pre-cooked, I don't want it."

The waiter shook his head. "No, we don't do that here."

"How 'bout the clams? They outta the can? 'Cause if you bring me a dish with clams outta the can, I'm gonna send it back."

The waiter waved his hand from side to side. "All our seafood is fresh off the boat."

An older man, wearing thick black horn-rimmed glasses, approached with a pitcher of water. He reached for Benny's glass.

Benny raised his hand. "*Stop.*"

"*Aqua minerale, Signore?*" the waiter asked.

"Mhm," Benny grunted.

"*San Pellegrino?*"

Benny shook his head, "*Fiuggi,*" he shouted. "The green bottle. No gas."

The waiter glanced at the busboy and jerked his head toward the kitchen. The man rushed off.

Benny looked at Nicky. "Carbonation upsets my stomach."

"No shit? Thought it would help you digest." There was hope that Nicky would not experience the combustible potion of Benny's internal wind and the green *Polo*.

"Gentleman," the waiter interrupted. "Would you like to hear our specials?"

"Tell the chef to make us whatever he wants," Benny said.

The waiter cleared his throat. "Well, *signore*. He can make you anything, but how does he know what *you* want?"

"Fish," Benny barked. "Bring us some fish."

"*Si, Signore.*" The waiter ran off.

"Surprise 'em like that and you know it'll be fresh."

Nicky pursed his lips, raised his eyebrows and nodded.

"Gotta go wash up," Benny said. "Make some room, too. Gimme a chance to see the kitchen. We can always leave if it don't look good." He disappeared down a narrow hallway.

Nicky checked his watch.

"*Fiuggi, Signore.*" The busboy filled each glass, placed the bottle in the center of the table and rushed off.

Nicky glanced over at the family enjoying lunch. He grinned as he watched the mom help her daughter spin a forkful of spaghetti. The little girl turned and smiled. Nicky gave her a thumbs up.

BANG. A thunderous clap rang out across the room. Nicky spun around directing his gaze toward the bathroom.

Benny slowly emerged from the dark corridor.

Nicky's eyes locked on him as he approached.

Benny stopped.

Nicky stiffened and reached for his ankle.

Benny glanced over his shoulder, slowly reached around his waist and picked his pants out of his ass crack.

Nicky sat back and let out a breath.

Benny fell into his chair and took a drink of water. "They gotta fix that door to the shithouse."

"You see the kitchen?"

"Yeah, looks fine. Clean." Benny loosened his collar and tucked his napkin into his shirt.

"How you know so much 'bout restaurants?" Nicky scraped the dirt from under his fingernails with his butter knife.

"First job before I got mixed up in our business. Worked in my brother's deli. Used to make sangwiches. Five bucks a pop. Good business."

"Your brother got a deli?"

"Had. Burned down. Needed cash to pay his vig. Had no choice."

Nicky pursed his lips and nodded.

The busboy placed a basket of bread on the table.

"Hey, guy," Benny said. "Tell your boss 'bout the door to the outhouse back there."

The man smiled and ran off.

Benny frowned. "Crazy bastard has no idea what

I'm talkin' 'bout. Careful with that door in case ya gotta shit later."

Nicky flashed the thumbs up sign.

"Where was I?"

"Your brother torched the deli."

"Right. That's where I met The Snake. He had a caterin' truck. Used to buy shit from us. After the fire, my brother went partners with him. Next thing I know, I'm workin' with the stars."

"Stars?"

"Yeah, ya know, movie stars. Had an in with the Teamsters. Used to give the guy an envelope. When they made movies in Philly, we'd sell 'em food. Right there on the street. Got to meet Rocky. Never forget it."

"You met Rocky?"

Benny pursed his lips and nodded. "Got his signature. Hanged it in my den," he said, beaming with pride.

"There ya go."

"Those were the days. Was already married, but Jesus, man, you shoulda seen the broads. Runnin' 'round half naked in their unde'wears like it's their regular clothes." Benny raised his napkin and wiped the sweat from his brow.

Nicky pursed his lips and nodded.

"Good money, too. Ripped off the movie people. Charged 'em twenty bucks for a sangwich, not five like in the deli. They didn't care. They build it into the ticket prices. That's how that business works."

"Twenty bucks, eh? That's a lot for a sangwich."

"Yeah but the problem was we got paid by check. Gotta declare that. Got no choice. End a the day," Benny raised his right hand, placed his fingertips under his chin pointing to his neck and flicked them out towards Nicky, "You got *UGATZ*—nuttin'. Couldn't stuff the cash in your pocket like we was doing at the deli."

"Still sounds like a money maker. Twenty bucks."

"Didn't last long. My brother ran it into the ground. Too busy chasin' broads."

Nicky grunted. "Sounds like that punk, Arnie."

"*HEY*," Benny barked. "Watch what ya say 'bout the boss' kid." He glanced over his shoulder. "Can't help it. Takes after the old man. Besides, you're one to talk."

Nicky shrugged.

"*Frutti di Mare*," the waiter announced, placing a dish in front of Benny.

Benny looked down suspiciously.

The busboy slid a plate in front of Nicky and darted off.

"Linguine with clams and mussels," the waiter said. "Enjoy." He marched away.

Benny's eyes narrowed. He reached over and stuck his fork into Nicky's dish. "I gotta pick."

"Help yourself."

"Try some a this," Benny said.

"Nah. Don't like tentacles. Give me nightmares."

"Pasta's hard."

Nicky grunted. He tore off a chunk of bread, soaked up some sauce and stuffed it in his mouth.

The busboy returned with a large peppercorn grinder. "Black pepper?"

"Too late. Already started eatin'." Benny shooed him away. "Gotta remember this place; if I'm ever up here again, that is." He raised his napkin and wiped his mouth.

"Why, this job we gotta do, you think we gotta come back?"

Benny shook his head. "Mhm-mhm. One shot deal." He reached for the bread, mopped up some broth and motioned for the waiter.

"Yes, *Signore*?"

Benny pointed to the basket. "Be kind. More bread. Gotta soak up the juice."

"*Si, Signore.*"

"You're gonna get grease on your shirt. You should wear your *mappine* like this. Understand?" He pointed to the napkin on his chest.

"I'm careful."

"You don't listen. I'm tellin' ya. You watch."

Nicky glanced down at his shirt. "No spots, see?"

Benny waved his hand dismissively. "I'm warnin' ya. Time we get outta here, it'll be blood red."

Nicky shook his head. "I'm careful."

"Careful, huh? Like when ya do your cuttin'?"

"Hm, Mh."

Benny snorted. "I know. You are pretty good with that blade. That's why Eddie wanted ya for this job. In and out. Quick and quiet." He shoveled a mountain of seafood into his mouth.

The busboy returned with more bread.

Nicky tore off a hunk and soaked it in a puddle of gravy. "Yeah, I know. In and out. Quick and quiet. You keep sayin' that. Don't know why."

"You'll find out," Benny said, reaching for the bread. "Don't worry. Just listen to me and everthin'll be okay."

Nicky shrugged.

"Been meanin' to ask ya somethin'?"

"G'head."

"You slice open that horse Eddie stuffed the guy inside of a few years back?"

Nicky shook his head. "Heard 'bout it, but no, before my time. Gotta say, pretty creative."

Benny scowled. "Ain't right."

"Why, too barbaric?"

"For the guy? No. The horse? Yeah. Ain't right."

Nicky pursed his lips and nodded.

"Who taught ya howta cut, Spics?"

"Mhm-mhm. Soul brother. Mack the Knife. Like the song, but he didn't cut no people. Only tires."

"Tires?"

"Met him when I worked at my uncle's station in North Philly when I was a kid. Car pull up, I'd pump gas, Mack cut tires. Pump and cut. Then we'd sell the *schmuck* a new set. Before self-service. Now ya can't make any money with gas. Oil companies run that racket."

"Your uncle still got the station?"

Nicky shook his head. "Jew landlord raised the rent. Uncle got pissed. Told him to fuck off. Heeb threw him out. Just as well, neighborhood went to shit."

"Make me unde'stand. This Mack guy. He showed ya how to use a blade?"

"Yeah, more less. I'd watch him real good. But one day, he came in all leanin' over. Talkin' funny. Arm hangin' down like this." Nicky scraped the floor with his hand.

Benny scowled. He made a fist and pointed his index and pinky finger. "*Malocchio?*"

"Evil eye?" Nicky shook his head. "Drunkard."

"*Ubriacone?*"

"Yeah, real lush. Kept a still in the woods. Possum jumped in one day and got cooked. Poisoned the hooch. Mack's liver burned up. Dropped dead. After that, I'd have to pump, and cut. Was a lotta work. Got in and out. Had to be quick. Quiet too." Nicky picked up his butter knife and thrust it forward in a quick short burst. "Like that."

With a curious look, Benny asked, "You left-handed?"

"Mhm. Why?"

"No reason. You twirl your pasta with your right, but ya was holdin' the knife with your left."

"Mother taught me how to twirl spaghetti with my right. Said it'd be easier."

"Always cut a guy the same way?"

Nicky shook his head. "'Pends on the job. Sometimes I look for an organ. Other times I might slice him open up to his throat. Bleeds more that way."

"How ya decide?"

"How much time I got. How much trouble he gives me. That's why I keep askin' ya bout this job. Gotta know how I need to work."

"In and out. Quick and quiet. No noise. That's all ya gotta know. Just listen to me."

Nicky nodded. "What about you? You always shoot a guy in the foot first?"

"'Pends. If he annoys me, yeah. That way, I make him suffer. Got no choice. But it's always easier to simply put a bullet into the back of their head."

"Easier for who? You or them?"

"Both. More humane that way, no? When they ain't expectin' it."

Nicky pursed his lips and nodded. "You always use a gun to do a job?"

"Most the time. If noise is gonna be a problem, I'll

toss him off a roof. Lead him up there like we gonna kill some other poor bastard." Benny raised his fat palm and squeezed. "Then I crush the guy's balls. Knock the wind outta him. Once he loses his breath, I throw him over the side."

"What if he don't die?"

"They always die."

"What if he lives?"

"Always pick a buildin' high enough so they can't survive the fall."

"What if he screams? Ya said ya do it that way when ya can't make noise."

Benny raised his palm and clenched his fist again. "That's why ya crush their nuts. Can't speak. Takes away their vocal ability like ya got a pillow over their face. Feels like their drownin'."

Nicky raised his eyebrows, pursed his lips and nodded.

"Let me ask ya somthin'?" Benny said. "When ya gotta cut a guy, ever wonder if it's the right thing to do? Ya know, if he deserves it or not?"

"Mhm, Mhm. Figure if I been sent to get him, he's gotta be a piece a shit. More'n likely deserves it. Just do my business and don't even think 'bout it. Tomorrow's anothe' day. How 'bout you? Ya shoot a guy in the foot or toss him off a roof, ya ever think ya shouldn't have?"

"Don't think about it. Just do what I'm told. Got no

choice. Learned that a long time ago." Benny pushed his plate forward.

"There ya go." Nicky slid his plate toward Benny's and looked down. "See," he said, pointing to his shirt. "No grease."

Benny grunted.

"*Finito*?" the waiter asked.

Nicky nodded. "What ya got for dessert?"

"*No dessert*," Benny snapped. "Just the check."

The waiter ran off.

Nicky pressed his right thumb against his other four fingers and waved his hand at Benny. "*Che cazzo*! What the fuck? Why can't we have some dessert? Ya said yourself, we got time."

"Not here. I know a place up the street. You'll see."

Nicky pursed his lips, raised his eyebrows and nodded.

. . .

Benny stepped out of the pastry shop carrying a small white box. "Follow me. Someone I want ya to meet." He took six steps and stopped.

Nicky glanced up at the ornate black and white sign swinging over the sidewalk. "Caffe' Victoria?"

"*Vittoria*. No C, two T's and cash only. That's how ya know it's good."

"I thought it was good if it didn't smell."

"That's restaurants. This here's a bar. Old time bar. Mainly for espresso. No drunks. Mr. Clean don't put up with that shit."

"Mr. Clean, huh? I gotta see this Mr. Clean."

"C'mon," Benny said. "Ya won't regret it."

A tall bald man in a skin-tight T-shirt stood behind the counter pumping a giant brass espresso machine. A gold hoop hung from his left ear and giant tattoos covered his enormous biceps. "What can I get ya, buddy?" he asked, looking at Benny.

"Two espressos, long."

"*Lungo.* You got it, buddy." He placed a cup under the portafilter spout and reached for the long handle.

Benny motioned toward Mr. Clean and whispered, "That's how ya make espresso."

Nicky pursed his lips and nodded. "Somethin' tells me that's not how he got those biceps."

Mr. Clean set down two cups. "Enjoy."

Nicky followed Benny to a table at the back of the empty coffee shop, twice glancing over his shoulder.

Like a kid on Christmas morning, Benny tore open the small white box. "*Lobster tails*," he said, with a look of excitement. He stuffed a paper napkin into his collar and chomped on the narrow end of the curved pastry. A wad of cream dribbled down his chin.

"Sounds crunchy," Nicky said. He reached for the other treat.

Benny nodded while he chewed. With a full mouth, he mumbled, "Hard on the outside, soft on the inside."

"Like a real lobster. But first ya gotta trap 'em and then steam 'em. Make 'em sweat." He bit into the delicacy.

"Watch your shirt."

Nicky waved his hand dismissively.

Benny shook his head in disgust.

Out of the corner of his eye, Nicky spotted someone enter through the front door. He spun around. A young woman with long dark hair, wearing round mirrored sunglasses and dressed in a tight black minidress and stilettos, stepped into the café. She slipped off her shades, leaned over the bar and gave Mr. Clean a long French kiss.

"Relax, will ya," Benny said.

Nicky laughed. "That must be Mrs. Clean."

Benny frowned.

. . .

"C'mon, there's one more stop we gotta make before the job." Benny charged forward into the street.

"*BENNY, look out*," Nicky shouted.

A black BMW with tinted windows screeched to a halt. The driver, a young bearded man in a blue track suit, laid on the horn, stuck his head out the window and lit into Benny with a stream of Italian profanities.

Benny stared him down.

"What the fuck ya doin?" Nicky asked. "You wanna get yourself killed, or somethin'?"

"I knew he'd stop. Bastard had no choice."

Nicky looked around. Tourists stopped, pointed and a few began filming with their phones. "I think we got a problem."

"Relax. No cops."

"Not yet. What 'bout that guy?"

"What 'bout him?"

"Wanna rough him up?"

"Fuck him." Benny raised his middle finger at the driver. "Let's go."

The dark sedan tore off down Hanover Street.

"Where we goin', now?" Nicky asked. "Got all this time, we coulda stopped at those casinos."

"No time. In and out. Quick and quiet. Gotta take care a somthin' before the job."

"You got someone else ya want me to meet?"

Benny shook his head. "Gotta pick somethin' up."

"We need the bag?"

"Don't need the bag."

Nicky pursed his lips and nodded.

Benny picked up his pace.

Nicky trailed a few steps behind. He assumed the adrenaline cocktail of caffeine and sugar must've put a fire in the old man's step.

Without warning, Benny made a sharp left and darted down a long dark ally.

Nicky froze. He peered between the two brick buildings. Glancing over his shoulder, satisfied he wasn't being tailed, he cautiously followed. Thirty feet in, Benny disappeared inside an open doorway.

Nicky slowly stepped through the entrance, descended the short flight of stairs and looked around. He found himself in a subterranean panetteria. An assortment of fresh baked artisan breads lined a metal wire rack by the door. A small display case to the left contained personal pizzas, cookies and a variety of focaccias. The warm scent of yeast filled the low-ceilinged basement, covering him like a cozy blanket on a cold winter morning.

"Lunch, pastry, coffee and now bread?" Nicky asked. "We workin' or we on a food tour? What kinda job is this, anyway?"

"In and out. Quick and quiet. Don't worry 'bout it. Just listen to me."

Nicky sighed. "Okay, but I been listenin' all day and all I know is I'm in a crypt surrounded by baked pizza dough."

Benny pointed to the shelf. "See that?"

Nicky nodded. "I see that."

"That's the real thing. Not like the shit ya get in stores back home. Know why?"

Nicky shrugged.

Benny furrowed his eyebrows. "Water."

Nicky raised his eyebrows. "It ain't polluted?"

"Nah. Somethin' 'bout the pipes. Filters it real good. Then ya mix it with this yella powder. They call it, *SEMOLINA*. And ya don't pump no air into the loafs. Bake 'em in a coal fired oven. Makes 'em smoky. Been here before. I don't bring my wife some, I'm a dead man."

Nicky pursed his lips and nodded. "Gotta hand it to ya, Benny. Ya know 'bout restaurants, ya know 'bout lobster tails, ya know 'bout coffee and now ya 'splainin' me 'bout bread. It's a wonder ya been mixed up in our business all these years."

Benny squinted. "What can I say, right? Gotta pay the bills, ya know what I mean?"

"I know what ya mean."

"Stick with what ya do best, that's what I say."

"Killin' people?"

"Takin' care a things. Like when I was in the deli, I took care a things. Got things done. That's why Sal took a likin' to me. Eddie, too."

Nicky looked around. "Just me and you down here or what? Nobody workin'?"

"Relax. Somebody be out soon. You watch. Like I said, I been here before."

Nicky pursed his lips and nodded.

Almost on cue, a tall dark-haired man dressed in a white T-shirt and chef's pants slowly stepped out from behind a wall of flour sacks. A half Venetian brown leather masquerade mask covered the right side of his face. "Be righta wit' you," he said, in a thick Italian accent. He scraped up a pile of charcoal briquettes with an old-fashioned flat scoop shovel and tossed the fuel into the glowing firebox. Sliding a long wooden peel into the arched brick opening, he extracted several loaves.

Benny jerked his head toward the baker. "See that?

Nicky raised his eyebrows and nodded. "I see that."

"That's how ya make bread."

"Thought it was the water?"

Benny clenched his hands like he was gripping a billiard cue. "It's all in the arms and elbows." He thrust his fists forward and slightly drew them back. "Like shootin' pool."

"Looks more like a pizza maker."

Benny waved his hand forward dismissively. "Them are amateurs. This here guy is an artist."

"What happened to his face?"

Benny raised his index finger to his lips. He lowered his voice. "Got behind on his payments. Shylock shoved his head in the oven. Told him he had four days to bring his account current, otherwise he'd come back and throw the rest of him in."

Nicky pursed his lips and nodded. "So, he wears a mask?"

"He wears a mask."

"He ain't 'fraid he's gonna scare off customers with that thing on?"

"Got no choice. Would you buy bread from a guy who looks like the devil?"

Nicky raised his eyebrows, pursed his lips and shook his head.

. . .

The Coupe de Ville slowly rolled down the narrow tree-lined street. Spring flowers bloomed along the sidewalk.

"Ya sure we're not lost?" Nicky asked.

"Not lost." Benny pointed. "There. Pull over. We're early."

Nicky parked behind a windowless white van. "This don't look like Boston."

"They call it *Cambridge*."

"How long we gotta wait?"

"Not long. In and out. Quick and quiet."

"Then we head back?"

"Then we head back."

"Gonna be a long drive."

Benny grunted.

"Maybe we stop at those casinos on the way home."

"No time."

Nicky motioned toward the back seat. "Had time for some bread."

"Told ya, already. Didn't bring that home, I'd be a dead man."

"Guy gave me the creeps."

"On account a the mask?"

"The whole story. Reminds me when I was a kid."

"How so?"

"Parents used to fight like wild animals. One night, my old man tried to stuff my mother in the oven. First time I pulled a knife."

"Ya cut him?"

"Didn't have to. Bastard let her go. Packed up his shit and ran off. Never saw him again."

"She have to wear a mask after that?"

Nicky shook his head. "Got there just in time. Little sunburned, but her face didn't melt. Might've been why she got skin cancer though."

"Sorry to hear that."

Nicky cracked open the window. The green *Polo*—now infused with the aroma of warm yeast—was coming on strong. He drew in a long breath of fresh air, leaned back and closed his eyes. "Gotta get some rest. That meal filled me up."

"Don't get too comfortable. Gotta go to work soon."

"Don't worry. I'll be ready. That's why Eddie told ya to bring me. Knows he can count on me."

"That's why, huh?"

Eyes closed, Nicky pursed his lips and nodded.

"Like I said, don't get too comfortable."

Nicky felt the car slightly rock. He peered under his eyelids.

Benny reached around his huge waist and pulled out a .38 revolver from under his suit jacket. With a flick of the wrist, he flipped open the cylinder and checked his ammo.

Nicky's heart raced. He sat upright. "Thought ya said we gotta be quiet."

"We do. Just makin' sure this thing is ready in case there's any surprises."

"What kinda surprises?"

"Surprises." Benny leaned forward and slid the pistol under his seat.

A young pregnant woman with short blonde hair slowly jogged by. Her eyes shielded by dark sunglasses, she glanced back at the car as she approached the intersection. Nicky focused one eye on the girl and kept the other on Benny.

Benny stared out the front windshield watching her as she turned right at the corner and disappeared behind a hedge. He checked his watch. "She's early."

Dumfounded, Nicky asked, "Who's early?"

"Arnie's whore. She's early. C'mon, let's take care a this thing and get home."

"What are ya talkin' 'bout? Ya tellin' me I gotta cut a broad? I don't do that."

Benny's face tightened. "Just listen to me, awright, and everything'll be okay."

"I been listenin' to ya all day and I still don't know what's goin' on." Nicky raised his voice. "Ya tell me I gotta cut some whore who don't look like no whore and I say *I WANNA KNOW WHAT THE FUCK IS GOIN' ON!*"

"Keep ya voice down, will ya?" Looking defeated, Benny shook his head and sighed. "Arnie meets this college chick in a bar. From England. They call 'em *exchange students*. Knocks her up. Tells her he'll pay for an abortion. She says no. Wants a kid. He don't want no kid. Eddie finds out. Orders his son to convince her to leave the kid and get lost. Wants to be a grandpa. Girl tells Arnie she's havin' the kid and goin' back to England. So Eddie sends us up here to take care a things. Had no choice. Said ain't no whore gonna steal his grandkid. Got it? Now, let's go."

Nicky scowled. "Look, Benny. I don't cut women and I definitely ain't gonna cut no baby. That's Charles Manson shit. Ain't my thing."

"Who said anythin' 'bout cuttin' a baby? That's why Eddie told me to take ya. The baby's comin' back with us. Got some blankets and shit in the bag. Wife packed it for me."

Speechless, Nicky stared straight ahead.

"What's the problem? Ya said yourself ya don't think about it when ya gotta cut someone."

"This is different."

"Look. Eddie tells me to do somethin', I do it. Don't ask no questions." Benny's eyes narrowed. "And neither do you."

"*FUCK YOU AND FUCK EDDIE*. I don't cut women and I ain't gonna cut out no baby. Tell that little shit Arnie to come up here and do it."

Benny sighed. "Ya know, Nicky...sometimes, ya gotta do what ya don't always wanna do. Got no choice." He leaned forward.

The fat slug's hand didn't get past his knee before Nicky drove his four-inch out-the-front switchblade into Benny's abdomen. The large man shuddered. As he began to scream, Nicky cupped his right hand over Benny's mouth and dragged the blade up from the entry point below the small intestines into the ribcage. A mix of bodily fluids oozed from the gaping wound. Nicky pull out the knife, pushed Benny's head back and with one swipe, quickly and quietly sliced the sloth's throat from ear to ear. Blood spurted from his neck. Nearly decapitated, Benny's head slumped onto his chest. His crisp white shirt quickly and quietly turned a dark crimson red. Nicky reached back for the small bag.

. . .

It was just past midnight when Nicky pulled over. The remote street along the South Philadelphia waterfront was darker than the black water flowing down the Delaware River.

Parked in a secluded spot behind an abandoned building, surrounded by squalor, he looked around. The run-down neighborhood was deserted. Satisfied he was alone, Nicky grimaced, pointed the .38 at his left foot and fired.

. . .

"Funny," Eddie said, sitting behind his large walnut desk. "After a six-hour drive, seems like there'd be more blood on the driver's side carpet."

"Like I said, Eddie. I wrapped it real good.

Eddie pursed his lips, nodded and lit a cigarette. "All these years, never had a problem with him. Now I ask him to take care a this, and the old bastard turns cold when he gets a look at that whore. Goddamn shame." Eddie took a drag.

The Virgin, hands folded at his waist, stood expressionless to Eddie's right. The Snake, equally stone faced, flanked his left.

Nicky pursed his lips and nodded. "Couldn't finish the job after I cut him. Had no choice. Didn't know if I could make it back with a hole in my foot. Wouldn't want to get stopped and have a cop start askin' questions. Baby be layin' there cryin', bags a hot bread in the back seat, Benny rolled up in in blankets in the trunk."

Eddie blew out a cloud of smoke. "I unde'stand. Ya did the right thing. Benny didn't do the right thing. Fat fuck. Tried to stop ya by shootin' ya in the foot." He turned toward The Snake and shook his head.

"When that girl heard the shot, she turned and ran. Even with a bun in the oven. Thought 'bout finishin' the job, but figured I'd never find her."

Eddie nodded. "Checked with a guy I know up there. Said she skipped town. No sign of her. Apartment's empty." He leaned forward, narrowed his eyes and lowered his voice. "Almost like someone tipped her off."

Nicky kept one eye on Eddie and the other on The Virgin.

With a look of disgust, Eddie waved his hand forward dismissively and sat back in his chair. "Fuck it." He wagged his finger. "Still…gotta wonder why there wasn't more blood on the driver's side. Six hours an awful long way to go with a bullet in your foot. Even wrappin' it up real good." He glanced back at The Virgin.

Nicky's boss didn't move.

"Took some pills. Keep 'em in the glove box for hangovers."

Eddie raised his eyebrows, pursed his lips and

nodded. "Take some time off. Heal that foot. Probably gonna have to find ya some other work. Gonna have a limp. Not gonna be able to balance. Might not be able to cut anymore."

Nicky raised his eyebrow and nodded. "Might not."

"Don't worry. We'll take care a ya. *You* did the right thing.

Driving in Silence

Nino DePasquale glanced at his watch, turned to Dino—his fraternal twin brother—and jerked his head to the left. The two men, known on the street as "The Silencers", stepped into the dimly lit shop just off Atwells Avenue. Carmen "The Cheese Man" Pistone didn't open for business until he took care of *Business*.

Nino's dark eyes adjusted to the room's low lighting while his olive toned skin absorbed the dampness. He wrinkled his nose as the aroma of sweaty feet enveloped him. August mornings in New England were hot, and the recent heat wave made it even worse. Despite the building's use as a dairy product production facility, the old structure lacked air conditioning. The humid muggy air mixed with the dry, pungent odor of a variety of aging cheese produced a suffocating cloud of noxious fumes.

Wearing a white water-soaked apron, Providence, Rhode Island's biggest bookie, measured in pounds and winnings, emerged from the back room.

Nino wondered if the moisture was from cheese-water or the sweat that oozed out of Carmen's fat.

"*Nino, Dino*," Carmen roared.

Nino waved.

The short plump Sicilian dried his hands on the back of his pants. "Perfect timing. Was about to take a shit before starting the next batch. Hang on a sec'." He disappeared behind a yellowed transparent plastic shower curtain. "Gotta go to the *bacous!*" he sang.

The last person Nino heard refer to a bathroom as an outhouse using old-country slang was his paternal grandfather, Giuseppe DePasquale. Nino turned to his brother and smiled.

Dino frowned.

Carmen grunted. "You guys have breakfast yet? Just made a batch of fresh mozzarella. Help yourself. Doc says I gotta lay off the dairy. Bad for my colitis."

Dino threw up his hands in disgust. He reached into

a water tank, grabbed a soft white ball and bit into it like an apple.

Nino peered inside the large steel container. Hearing the toilet flush, he thought twice about sampling the *Bufala*.

Carmen returned, stuck his hands in a vat of white curds and began massaging the goop. "Look at ya. Matching double breasted suits, thin silk ties, fitted white shirts. And the black leather boots; ya get any pointier than that, ya gotta go to Cuba. Best dressed mutes around. Who'd think youse was a couple a psychopaths. Couldn't run my business without ya. Wouldn't trade ya for the best killers this side of Sicily."

Dino smiled.

"Love the slicked back hair. Not like me." Carmen patted his head. "Cue ball. Olive oil?"

Dino gave the rotund fromager a thumbs up.

Despite their inability to verbally communicate, the brothers had developed a good rapport with the slimy grease ball. They understood the language of "*The Black Hand*" and most importantly, "*Omertà*"— the oath of silence; in their case, literally. And like all Italians, they spoke the sign language of the old country. Business details were seamlessly conveyed using hand gestures, body motions and facial expressions.

Still, Nino was always careful when accepting one of Carmen's contracts. Approaching forty, the brothers worried that the window of opportunity to make a step up in the underworld was closing. Each new assignment was viewed strategically. Would it be more productive to perhaps take Carmen out versus the target? Were there broader implications to wiping out the intended victim? Might the deceased's family or cohorts seek retribution and demand the brothers' heads? And lastly, could Carmen be trusted? With a reputation for turning on his colleagues for no reason, there was always the chance that they could walk into a setup. Things they might've taken for granted in their youth now were given more consideration.

While increasingly wary, in the end, Nino and Dino knew they had to make a living. With a client base that spanned New England, the uncouth bookmaker kept them busy and more importantly, he paid C.O.D.— *Cash on Death*. Nino looked at his customer and jerked his head up.

"Yeah, right," Carmen said. "Let's get down to business." He sat down at the small table in the middle of the room and held up a large manila envelope.

Nino reached for it.

"Hang on a sec'. Let me 'splain."

Dino, hands folded together at his waist, stood a step behind his brother to the left.

Carmen pulled out a black-and-white photograph. "This piece a shit needs to go bye-bye." He raised his hand and waived by raising and lowering his fingers. "It's that simple. Stiff owes me lotsa coin. Gave him plenty a chances to make me whole. Skipped town. Tired of his horseshit. I want him whacked. No good for business. *Capiche?* Understand?"

Nino nodded.

Dino flashed the okay sign.

"Good." Carmen handed Nino the package. "Everything ya need to know is in there: Picture, known aliases, relatives and a map. I gave ya a list of a few guys that can help. Our kind. Most owe me a favor. They should be able to clue you in on how to find him; point you in the right direction. I heard he headed west. Other side of Connecticut. Bit of a drive, but you'll find the bastard." Carmen stood up and returned to massaging his curds. He glanced back. "And when ya do, make sure he knows I sent youse."

Nino raised his eyebrows.

Carmen stopped manipulating the whey. "Oh, yeah, right. How ya' gonna tell him being mute and all." He thought for a moment. "I got it." He pulled a wad of cheese from the water, plopped it into a plastic container and dropped it in a small clear bag. He handed it to Nino. "Take this. By the time you get there, in this heat, it'll spoil. Before you kill him, you shove that ball of rotten cheese in his mouth until he chokes. He'll know who sent ya."

. . .

Nino checked his watch. As noon approached, the mid-day sun heated up the interior of the red Jeep Liberty.

Dino steadily navigated the SUV down the interstate.

Catching his brother's attention, Nino pointed to the speedometer.

Dino nodded, eased off the gas and glided into the travel lane.

With a lengthy rap sheet, Nino didn't want to risk being pulled over. The brothers were well known among law enforcement; local, state and federal. The two-hour drive from Providence had been hot. Despite the stifling heat, and preferring fresh air, Nino chose an open window over the vehicle's air conditioning. He glanced back at the bag of cheese and wondered how long it would take for the decomposition to begin.

As his brother stoically drove, Nino studied the contents of the manila envelope. The man in the photograph was tall and lean with a pointy nose and a dark bubble perm. He wore a large diamond stud in his left ear. From the sign in the background, it appeared he was exiting the Twin Rivers Casino. Nino concluded he was packing by the slight bulge visible around his ankle. One hundred miles west of Providence, he glanced down at the map, tapped his brother's arm and pointed to the exit.

Dino steered off the highway and pulled into a small plaza. Porto "The Bagel Man" Guomo, owner of Armenia Bagels and Deli, was the first name on Carmen's list.

Despite being lunchtime, the sandwich shop was empty. Wire bins filled with assorted bagels lined the back wall and a life-size plush pink panther from the cartoon series—with one eye missing—hung from the ceiling. A gruff looking unshaven man leaned over the counter smoking a cigarette. He glanced up at the sound of the door opening.

"Hey. You must be those mutes Carmen told me 'bout. Come on in. I'm Porto." He took a drag on his cigarette and blew a cloud of smoke into the rack of bagels. "I'd offer you some a those bread donuts but they been sittin' there a few days. They just there for show. Ya know what I mean. That wasn't a question."

Nino nodded. While not sure what Porto's racket was, any connection with Carmen spelled scumbag. Whatever his vice, Nino hoped he could quickly point them to the target so they could get home. From the little he saw so far on the drive in, if there was any city more depressing than Providence, it was Waterbury.

"Carmen told me you might need help lookin' for someone. Cheese Man and I go way back."

Nino slid the photo across the counter.

Porto glanced down, took a final drag and stamped

the cigarette out on the picture. "Saw him a few days ago. Said he was passin' through, but I knew he was lyin'."

Nino leaned forward and peered into Porto's eyes.

The Armenian's gaze nervously shifted between the brothers and the front door.

Nino glanced over his shoulder. Catching Dino's attention, he arched one eyebrow and turned back toward Porto.

"Every piece a shit known to mankind passes through this town," Porto said. "The worst ones stick around and run for office. Pedophiles, extortionists, mayors, governors. All a buncha shitbags."

Losing patience with the history lesson, Nino pointed at the black-and-white image.

"Heard enough, eh? Okay. My sources tell me he hangs out at Mr. Sunshine's, the strip club. Took a likin' to a dancer. Real pig." Porto's eyes shifted toward the ceiling.

Nino glanced up at the pink panther and watched as air from the HVAC duct slowly spun it in circles.

"Big nasty mole on her ass. Got a hair or two stickin' out of it."

Nino grabbed the photo, glanced at Dino and headed for the door.

As Dino turned the ignition key, Nino saw Porto lower the blinds and flip the door sign so it read CLOSED. A black sedan with tinted windows pulled in as the brothers exited the plaza. Nino glanced in the passenger's side mirror. A tall blonde man entered the shop.

. . .

Nino's nostrils absorbed the putrid scent of stale beer, possibly mixed with a stew of dried bodily fluids that would illuminate like fire under a black light. Eighties heavy metal roared from speakers suspended over a brightly lit elevated linoleum dance floor. Small paper bowls of mixed nuts sat evenly spaced across the narrow ledge bordering the performance platform. Torn vinyl couches lined the back wall below an aluminum framed letter-board menu. Other than an elderly Asian man sipping a pint, the seedy nightclub was empty. Nino had frequented the worst of Providence's trashy strip joints, but this place beat them all.

A heavy man with long kinky hair, a rubber band cinching his goatee, stood behind the bar. He was dressed in a black burlap tunic that reached his knees over black track pants. "Hey, fellas," he shouted over the music in an Eastern European accent. "Come in, come in. I get you drink. We got broads too. You come in, yes? I am Balto."

Nino pointed to the stage.

"Of course. You watch naked whores and I bring you drinks. They be out soon. Almost time."

Nino turned to his brother, shrugged and headed

for the center of the room. He grabbed a chair across from the other patron. One by one, the senior citizen carefully lined up a row of foreign currency on the ledge in front of him.

Dino sat down, slid his glasses into his blazer pocket and smiled. He tossed a handful of nuts into his mouth.

Balto banged on the dressing room door. "Let's go," he barked. "Get out here and sell some booze." He waddled over, stood behind the brothers and placed his hands on both of their shoulders. "What I bring you to drink? Beer, whiskey, vodka? Vodka is my favorite."

Dino raised his thumb.

Balto patted him on the back. "Good choice. I bring you my best vodka." He headed back to the bar.

A young blonde and a mature brunette, both with their share of miles on them, stepped onto the stage. A tight white tank top covered the younger dancer's small breasts. She slipped off her G-string and strutted toward the old man. As the beat dropped, she squatted and doused the front of her shirt with his beer. The yellow man's slanted eyes widened to large wide circles. As she began to wildly thrust her pelvis to the music, he tossed a fistful of money at her.

"That's it," Balto roared. "Whore it up for the Commie Chink bastard."

The older woman removed her tattered pink bikini top, slipped off a stained white thong and tossed both in the brother's direction. Wearing only red platform stilettos, the effects of time and gravity were obvious as she vigorously jumped in place. She spun around, bent over, and grabbing both ass cheeks, spread her crack wide open.

Nino spotted a large mole on her right side.

Gazing at Nino between her legs, she ran her tongue over her lips.

Nino raised one eyebrow.

The dancer straightened, turned and slithered over.

Balto returned and set down two glasses. "First one on the house." He leaned over and lowered his voice to a whisper. "Be careful. That one got dirty ass." He stood up and pointed. "*You got dirty ass, today?*" he shouted. "You better be clean for these customers. They don't want to smell dirty ass."

Alternating both of her raised middle fingers to the rhythm of the music, the nude woman thrust her hairy groin toward Balto and mouthed, "Fuck you."

"*Fuck you, too. DIRTY ASS!*"

The woman turned and slapped her behind. She fell to the floor and backed up to within an inch of Nino's face.

Holding his breath, Nino focused on the large brown circle of raised flesh. As she rolled onto her back, he studied it closer. A long hair stuck up from its core. Her legs spread eagle to the sky, Nino turned to Dino and grimaced.

After what seemed like an eternity, she sat up and leaned forward. "Hi, boys. I'm Cloe. How are you both, today?"

Dino gave her the thumbs up sign.

Nino smiled.

"Glad to hear it," she said. "That's okay if you don't want to tell me your names. Most guys don't. Afraid I might look them up or tell their wives that they come here. When they do tell me their name, they lie. Like me, my name isn't Cloe, it's Veronica. And I'm not really a brunette I'm a red head." She laughed. "But you probably guessed that."

Nino assumed Veronica was in her sixties. While heavily made up, she wasn't half bad given how many times she'd likely been around the block. He reached into his jacket.

Veronica smiled. "I'd ask you to slip it into my garter but I'm not wearin' one." She giggled. "How 'bout this, instead?" She pressed her droopy mammaries together and leaned forward.

Nino wedged the black-and-white photo between what he guessed were DD cups.

Veronica glanced down, frowned and released her cleavage. Despite a fairly tight body for her age—without the benefit of augmentation—her National Geographic-like udders swung open like clappers in a church bell sending the picture sailing to the floor.

Nino reached forward.

"Hey, no touchin'" Balto shouted from the bar. "Even dirty ass."

Nino held up the photo.

"What do you want with that asshole?" Veronica asked.

"No lovey, love on the dance floor," Balto barked. "You want to make lovey, love? Get a room."

Nino unfurled a roll of bills and peeled off two twenties.

Veronica smiled. "I knew you had a wad in your pants."

"Tip or no tip," Balto yelled, "no playin' with the whores."

"Ignore that fat fuck. Just grab whatever you want." She turned to Dino. "You too, sweetie. Wanna cop a feel?"

Dino waved his hands from side to side.

She turned back to Nino. "No, huh?"

Nino pointed at the picture.

"I gotta say, you two are a couple a fuckin' weirdos." Veronica tucked the cash into her shoe. "He was here yesterday afternoon. Night before, too. Remember him because he had a pointy nose. Real pecker, pardon the pun. And that hair. Had a bush on his head that reminded me of the strawberry patch I had in the Seventies."

Dino grinned.

"Asked me if I wanted to go out after work. Said he had a room up the road. Not sure if it was the Red Bull or that rattrap down the hill."

Nino turned to his brother.

Dino glanced down at Carmen's list of names.

"Hey," Veronica snapped. "You wanna hear what I got to say or what?"

Nino nodded, pointed his index finger and rotated his wrist encouraging her to continue.

"So, I told him to go fuck himself. I don't do that kind of thing." She raised her leg high and slowly lowered it. "I'm a dancer," she said stylishly.

Nino expressed a skeptical "*Not*" face.

"Tried to impress me by sayin' he was a hitman for the mob. Sounded like he was bullshittin' me to try and get in my pants—even thought I wasn't wearin' any." Veronica giggled.

Nino shot his brother a look.

Dino arched one eyebrow.

"Said he was headin' to Hartford. Supposedly has a friend who is a big shot in the automotive industry. Had a job waitin' for him. That's why I figured he was blowin' shit up my ass about bein' an assassin. What kinda killer works in the car business?" She stood up. "Took a few bucks from him, let him squeeze my tits and off he went. Okay, time's up." She turned and headed toward the Chinaman.

Nino tucked the photo into his pocket.

The blonde dancer, now completely nude as well, slowly shimmied over.

Dino smiled.

Nino stood, tapped his brother on the shoulder and headed for the door.

. . .

After leaving Mr. Sunshine's, Nino and Dino grabbed a couple burgers at a nearby drive-in. Hopping back on the highway, Nino noticed a large steel crucifix overlooking the city. Based on what he learned about the area so far, he wondered if the cross was there to offer the local heathens a path to the Promised Land.

One exit up, perched high on a hill overlooking the interstate, the Red Bull Motor Inn could have served as the setting for a Seventies porno film. From its sultry neon sign to its dark wood exterior, the short-stay hostelry exuded a sleazy late-night ambiance.

Based on Veronica's tip, Nino thought it was worth making a quick pass through the property on the off chance they might spot the target. They surveyed the grounds and roamed the musty worn hallways. All they found were prostitutes, drug dealers and obvious undercover cops working vice. The latter led them to quickly move on, two exits east to the bottom of Wolcott Mountain.

. . .

As night fell, Dino steered the Jeep onto a dark street. More like a long driveway, crater size potholes and piles of trash haphazardly dotted the road. Slowly navigating the minefield, the brothers passed two abandoned homes. Without warning, the vehicle suddenly lurched to the right. Dino jerked the steering wheel in the opposite direction, but it was too late. The passenger's side front tire plunged into a deep black hole in the earth.

Nino gripped the dash. The SUV slowly careened forward eventually climbing back onto the roadway. Spotting a green neon *Motel* sign shaped like an arrow sticking up through overgrown grass, he pointed, motioning to Dino to park.

Nino jerked his head to the right, jumped out and led his brother up a flagstone path toward a small maroon house.

A large, round-faced, olive-skinned man with a black afro, wide fat nose and several days of stubble stood behind a screen-door. Barefoot, he wore an orange terry-cloth bathrobe. A black leather gun-belt slung low on his hips both secured the robe and holstered a small pearl handled revolver. A smoldering cigarette dangled from his left hand while his right rested on his pistol.

"You those maniacs Carmen told me to expect?" He took a long puff and blew a cloud of smoke through the screen.

Nino nodded and pointed to the list of names.

"Yeah, I'm 'Motel' Joe. Welcome to the Terrace Motel, or as most people call it, the 'Tear-Ass.' Come on in." A loud screeching wail screamed as he pushed open the rickety metal frame door.

Nino and Dino stepped into a small Sixties era wood paneled office. The room smelled like soggy cornflakes. A black and white television blared a late-night basketball game.

Holding his cigarette between his first two fingers, Joe pointed it toward a green love seat. "Make yourself comfortable." He fell into a shabby recliner and motioned toward the TV. "Sorry about the noise. Got a nickel on this and it ain't lookin' good."

Nino held up the photo.

"Right. So how you makin' out so far with that shitbag? Any luck?"

Dino folded his lips and shook his head.

"No surprise. He moves around. Makes an appearance here once a week. Shoulda been here by now. Usually needs a room for a few hours. You try the gentlemen's club other side of the mountain?"

Dino nodded.

"How about the whorehouse up the hill?"

Nino nodded.

Joe furrowed his brow. "Let me see that picture again."

Nino handed over the photo.

Joe put his cigarette out in a beanbag ashtray, slipped

on his reading glasses and carefully examined the image. He pointed. "What's this black spot next to his face?"

Dino pointed to the smoldering butt.

"Some people ain't got no class. Anyway, now that I'm lookin' at this, I just remembered somethin'."

Nino flipped his palms.

"His hair. Goes to a salon in the center of town. Likes to look good for the ladies. Cheese Man give you someone to see named Tony?"

Nino glanced down at the list and shook his head.

"Tony 'The Barber?'"

Nino rechecked the list and gave Joe the thumbs down.

"You sure? Maybe he made a mistake and wrote down Tony 'The Butcher,' Tony 'The Baker,' Tony 'The Brick Layer,' or Tony 'The Carpenter.'"

Growing tired of the name game, Nino silently sighed and scanned the entire page. Finding nothing, he flipped his palms and arched his eyebrows.

"Okay. Just want to make sure. Well, I don't want to tell you guys how to do your jobs, but it sounds like you ought to pay Tony a visit in the morning. Tony 'The Barber,' that is."

Nino looked at his brother.

Dino nodded.

Joe stood up and handed Nino the photo. "Tell you what. It's late. Let me give you guys a room for the night. On the house. You look wiped. Get a fresh start in the morning. Tony's place is just down the road. Tony 'The Barber.' Actually, all the Tony's are close by."

Nino gave Joe the thumbs up.

Joe tossed him a key. "Take room number seven. Maybe it'll bring me some luck with this game. You guys should have a quiet night. Most of hookers already turned their tricks and my kid won't be creepin' through your windows. He ain't into watchin' guys. More interested in the interracial stuff we got around here. Oh, and don't worry about gettin' robbed." Joe tapped his revolver. "I got that covered."

. . .

Nino slid the key into the lock and turned the handle. Nothing. He leaned his shoulder against the door and gently pushed. No success. Finally, he stepped to the side and turned to Dino.

His brother raised his right leg and with a spring like snap, drove his black leather boot forward. *BANG!* The old wood door rocketed open swinging wildly on its hinges. A potpourri of sour odors, along with a couple mice and a swarm of silverfish, escaped from the dank quarters. Dino stepped into the room and invited Nino to follow.

As he was about to enter, headlights lit up the parking lot. Nino glanced back toward the house. A car door closed. Peering through the blackness, he watched a lone figure slowly approach the office. The unknown visitor cast a tall shadow as they passed the walkway's lamp post. The screen door squealed. Concerned, Nino shot his brother a worried look.

Dino, already stretched out on one of the ratty twin beds, waved his hand forward dismissively.

. . .

After a late breakfast at a nearby truck stop, Nino and Dino headed toward the center of town. They arrived at the hair salon just as it was opening. They stepped inside and were surrounded by a jungle of potted plants. Nino wondered if he misread the sign out front and instead had walked into a florist shop. Spotting a stack of adult magazines in the waiting area, he knew they had the right address. He flipped the door sign around so it read *CLOSED*.

Dino picked up a tabloid and leafed through the pages.

"The ones that show the genitals are underneath," a short slim middle-aged man said, as he emerged from the back room. Dressed in a gold silk paisley shirt open to his navel, his chest completely hairless, black bellbottom slacks and leather sandals, he greeted the brothers with a salute. His dark hair was round and curly, and his eyebrows were pencil thin.

Dino crouched down and peered under the coffee table.

Nino caught his brother's gaze and shot him a dis-
approving look.

Dino frowned.

"You boys here for an early haircut? No need for an
appointment. I'm Tony, Tony 'The Barber.'" He patted
his vacant chair.

Dino pointed to the empty workstation to the left.

"Dave won't be in until noon. He likes to drink.
Takes him a while to get started in the mornin'."

Dino shook his head.

Tony grew agitated. "What the fuck? You guys a
couple a mutes or somethin?"

Dino nodded.

"You gotta be shittin' me, right?"

Nino shook his head.

"You really a couple a dumbies? Boy, this is gonna
be one of those days. Okay, like I said, Dave will be in
at noon if you wanna come back, or I can take a care
ya? So what's it gonna be?"

Nino held up the black-and-white photograph.

Tony squinted. "Hang on a second. Can't see a
fuckin' thing." He slipped on a pair of rose-tinted
Neostyle "Nautic 2" Elvis glasses.

Nino took note of Tony's long left pinky nail.

"What about him? I only cut his hair. And take
care a that thing for him." He pointed to a round red
toupee—fashioned in a bubble perm style—resting on

a canvas block mannequin head.

Nino looked at the hairpiece and studied the photo noticing, except for the color, it exactly matched Tony's hairstyle. He shot his brother a quick look.

Dino shrugged.

Tony pointed to his head. "Mine's the real thing. Dave gives me a permanent every few months. What hair your buddy in the picture has left is blonde. Guess it turns him on to be a redhead. Who the fuck knows. What someone does in the privacy of their own home is none a my business. God knows if people in this town knew what I do behind closed doors, they wouldn't be bringin' their kids in here to get their hair cut."

Nino pressed his right nostril closed, slipped his upside-down left pinky under the other side and snorted.

Tony laughed. "Yeah I do a little blow. Lot worse, too. I'd offer you some, but I need to restock my supply. Partied it all away last night."

Nino pointed to the photo.

"Comes in every few weeks." He motioned toward the wig again. "Got two a those. I swap them out every time he comes in. Likes me to air them out on the dummy for a while. No disrespect."

Dino shook his head.

"He was here a couple a days ago. Odd thing was, instead a havin' me glue his mushroom cap on his head like I normally do, he took it with him. Never did that before. Maybe he didn't want to be recognized. He's into some shady business, but like I said, I don't pry into my customer's lives. Ya know how it is. They sit there and talk and I just listen."

Nino glanced at Dino.

Dino raised his eyebrow.

"What are you guys, a couple a dope dealers? He owe you money or somethin'?"

Sensing Tony's fear, and growing tired of coming up empty at each stop along Carmen's scavenger hunt, Nino turned to Dino and bowed his head.

Dino opened his jacket exposing his shoulder holstered .357 Magnum.

Nino turned slightly to the side and lifted the back of his blazer. The grip of his Glock 37 poked out of his waistband.

Tony raised his hands. "Look, I don't want no trouble. You two lunatics got a beef with that guy, that's between youse and him. None a my business, right?"

Nino turned toward his brother hoping to sense his thoughts on how to proceed.

Before Dino could react, the shop's phone rang.

"Modern Hair Style, Tony 'The Barber' speaking."

Dino arched one eyebrow.

"Hey, how's it going…yeah, they're right here… yeah, that's fine. *Ohhhhh*, now I understand. Uh-huh… okay, got it." Tony hung up. "That was Joe. Told me the whole story. Why didn't ya tell me he sent you? Oh, right, never mind. No hard feelings, right?"

Nino nodded.

"Good, so, where were we?"

Nino pointed to the phone and flipped his palms.

"Joe said after you left this morning, he called around and confirmed what the stripper said. Sounds like we got a lot in common." Tony winked. "Anywhoski, your buddy's got a job waitin' for him in the capital city with a player in the auto business. He said there's a guy's name on Carmen's list—whoever the fuck Carmen is—that will be able to help you. Said it's the name with the asterisk next to it."

Nino glanced down at the page, looked at Dino and jerked his head toward the door.

· · ·

Forty minutes northeast of Waterbury, Hartford appeared to be another run-down New England eyesore. After a few wrong turns, Nino glanced down at the map and motioned for his brother to make a right. Halfway down the block he spotted a goofy looking man, talking to himself and pacing in front of an abandoned toilet at the corner of a four-way intersection. The wild haired man was dressed in a red flannel shirt and baggy blue trousers tucked into untied work boots. Nino directed Dino to pull over just short of the stop sign.

The eccentric pedestrian, head bowed and back hunched, shuffled toward the vehicle. Peering into the passenger's side window, he cocked his head and asked, "Who the fuck are ya, and what d'ya want? I'm Johnny." He jabbed his finger toward the right side of his face. "People used to call me 'One Eyed' Jack on account a my glass eye. Long story. Can't work. Just wander around all day. Everybody thinks I'm fucked up. Now they call me 'Crazy' Johnny on account a that politically correct bullshit. Whatever. No big deal. Fuck 'em."

Nino unfolded the map and maneuvered it into Johnny's field of view. Hoping he hit his mark, he jabbed his finger at the circle Carmen had drawn.

"Ya lost, eh?" He glanced at the front license plate. "Rhode Island, eh? What ya doin' in Connecticut?" He sucked in a massive amount of air, emitted a loud honking gurgle from the back of his throat and ejected a huge glob of sputum onto the sidewalk.

Nino grimaced.

As if a lightbulb went off, Johnny's eyes opened wide. "I get it. You those two wackos Carmen said to look out for. Musta told ya you'd find me on this street corner, eh?"

Nino nodded.

"I used to work for the man back in Providence. Long time ago. Would help him with the cheese. Before my health problems. Like I said, now I just amble about aimlessly like a nutcase. That's why they call me, 'Crazy' Johnny. You musta saw my nephew, Joe, before ya come lookin' for me, right?"

Intrigued to learn Johnny was Joe's uncle, Nino gave him the thumbs up.

"Joe and Carmen go way back. The motel man offered to be Carmen's muscle in exchange for wiping out his gambling debts. Offered to rub out a few guys no charge. *Gratis.* Carmen passed. Thought Joe was an out of control blowhard. Love the guy, he's family, but he's a bit of a hothead. Rumor is Carmen put a lien on the Motel instead. Not a good move. Place is a shithole. Worthless."

Nino stared blankly at Johnny.

"Musta ended up at Joe's on account a that stripper? Old redhead with the big cans? Hope ya didn't eat any a those bagels at that Muslim's place. Give ya the shits. God forbid I eat anythin' with seeds in it. Tear my colon to shreds. Bet Joe sent ya to see Tony, too. Tony 'The Barber'. Not the other ones in town. I ain't related to none of them. They're all nuts."

Nino politely smiled but was quickly losing patience with another history lesson. More unsettling was Johnny's ability to practically recount the brother's every move; the loon's insightfulness left him with an uneasy feeling.

"Don't talk much, eh? That's okay. Whatever."

Johnny sniffed. "*JESUS CRIPES!* What's that stench? Ya gotta corpse back there? Holy crap. I haven't smelled anthin' that bad since I shit my pants in the library."

Nino glanced over his shoulder at the bag of cheese. As bad as it smelled, he knew couldn't throw it in the trash. It was the only way to deliver Carmen's message. He turned back toward the window.

"Fuckin' hot out, no? Can't stand here all day. So, I guess if ya made it this far, ya must need somethin'?"

Nino questioned Johnny's choice of words regarding the length of their journey. He slowly nodded and held up the black-and-white photo.

"I can help ya, but what's in it for me? Like I said, I can't work on account a my eye." He pointed again. "Could use a few bucks. Ya know what I mean? So what d'ya say? Toss 'One Eyed' Jack some cash and 'Crazy' Johnny will help ya out."

Frustrated, Nino dug though his pocket and handed over a twenty.

"Cheap bastard." Jonny stuffed the bill in his shirt. Holding his nose, he stepped closer to the door to get a better look at the map. "Ya can throw that thing away. I'll tell ya where to go. Heard he's got a sponsor 'round here. Name is Larry. Bigshot in the automotive business. Real sleaze ball. People call him, 'The Weasel.' Got a thing for naked women. Who doesn't, right? Whatever. I couldn't get it up if ya shot me fulla elephant testosterone. Don't work no more. Nuttin' to do with my eye. Like I said, got some health problems. Whatever."

Nino frowned and pointed at his watch.

Johnny looked annoyed. "In a hurry, huh? Okay, whatever. Now listen. I'm only gonna say this once or else ya gonna have to pay me another twenty. Understand?"

Nino rolled his eyes and nodded.

"And I'm gonna warn ya. I'm sendin' ya to a real crummy part of town. Neighborhood's a real shithole. Worse than here."

Nino turned his palms up and shrugged.

"Don't care, eh? Okay, we'll see." Still hunched over, Johnny turned his body so it faced the intersection. He reached his left arm back level with his shoulder and awkwardly aimed his fingers toward the sky. Raising his head, he waved his right arm in a long arc and wiggled his fingers. Repeating the spasmodic choreography, he said, "Ya go that way, then turn. Past the empty lot. About a mile. That way, ya turn. Not before, but after. Follow the road. To the end. Can't miss the place. That way, turn and a mile. Got it?"

Confused, Nino looked at the intersection, glanced down at the map then turned toward Johnny.

The supposed hunchback stood up perfectly straight, spun around and ran. He disappeared behind an abandoned building.

Exasperated, Nino helplessly turned to his brother. Dino turned his palms up with a look of despair.

. . .

Dino parked the Jeep next to a white concrete block building.

Nino leaned out the window and looked up at the sign above an enormous mural of nude women. *Stripperz and Suckerz. We take it off and pull it out. Call us—we'll get it straight and get it off.*

Dino hopped out and headed around back.

Nino followed his brother through an open garage door. Posters of more naked women plastered the walls. A group of Hispanic men surrounded three box trucks.

A short pudgy man with curly dyed orange hair and large round glasses frantically scurried about. Dressed in tight beige slacks and brown leather ankle boots, he waved a clipboard in the air with one hand and pointed toward the three vehicles with the other. He calmed down when he noticed he had visitors.

"You guys want something?"

Nino pointed toward the trucks.

"Yeah, sure. Got a job for us. We can take care of it. Little busy right now, but come on in. I'm Larry, follow me."

Nino glanced at his brother.

Dino patted his shoulder holster confirming he was locked and loaded.

Larry led them to a small office with glass walls and invited them to sit.

Nino glanced over his shoulder and scanned the garage. The crew mingled about but didn't appear to be very engaged.

"Guatemalans. Lazy bastards. Fuckin' got a goldmine here, but these sons of bitches will kill me if I don't stay on top of them."

Dino slid the photo across Larry's desk.

Larry glanced down at the picture and frowned. "You lookin' for that asshole too? Let me know if you find him. Fronted him a few bucks and never saw him again. Promised he'd work it off for me but haven't seen him in months."

Nino's eyes narrowed.

"That's how it works in business. Sometimes you have to take your losses and move on. You guys look like a couple of players. Am I right?"

Dino shrugged.

"Okay, I get it. The strong silent type. That's okay, I don't mind doin' all the talkin'. Kind of like when I'm with my ladies." Larry flashed an evil grin.

Nino turned his palms over.

"Got an offer for you. Ever consider investing in a startup?"

Nino pointed his index finger and rotated his wrist motioning for Larry to explain. Maybe he would reveal a clue as to where they could find the target and close this assignment out. Then again, he sensed they were at a milestone that could make or break their whole relationship with Carmen. Feeling like the Cheese Man sent them on a wild goose chase, Nino had put his guard up wondering if they were walking into a trap.

"Good. Well here's the deal. I got somethin' real big I wanna show you." He snickered.

Nino glanced at Dino and furrowed his brow.

His brother nodded and rested his hand within easy reach of his pistol.

"This thing is gonna be huge. It'll make Hooters look like bush league. *IMAGINE*," Larry shouted, as he jumped from his chair and reached out his hands. "*Stripperz and Suckerz* in every major city across the country." He slowly rotated his body in a semi-circle gliding his hands as if he was crossing the continent. "Hot topless chicks working the production line instead of these Spics."

Dino gazed at the ceiling and stroked his chin.

"How 'bout I give you a tour? Show you my operation?"

Wearily, Nino nodded.

"Uh, actually, hang on a second. I need to make a quick call. Would you two excuse me for a second?"

The brothers stepped into the garage. Pacing, they watched as Larry pressed his cell to his ear, said a few words and walked out of his office. Nino sensed he had a nervous gait about him.

"C'mon. You're not gonna believe your eyes. Boy are you gonna be surprised." Larry approached a dented paneled truck.

"Here it is." Excited, he picked up a large cylinder-shaped device. The contraption resembled a vacuum cleaner with a buffing wheel attached to one end. "Technology before your eyes. And it's more than a machine; it's a *SYSTEM*. You saw the name out front, right?"

Nino nodded.

Larry puffed out his chest. "That was my idea," he said, beaming with pride. "Came up with it one night hanging out at the club. Was sitting there with my pants around my ankles and Heather under the table and it just came to me."

Nino glanced at his brother.

Dino rolled his eyes.

"Watch closely, boys." Holding his prized mechanical monster like a World War II era large-caliber machine gun, Larry flipped a switch. Loud honking squawks roared through the room. Intermittent pauses, accompanied by gasps of air, provided relief from the ruckus. Blasts of exhaust fumes blew out the rear of the device.

The Guatemalans hunkered down behind a dumpster. Nino shielded his eyes.

Larry's back arched as he struggled to steady the angry beast. As if hunting big game, he shoved his weapon into the truck, attacking the dents. Magically, the steel quickly restored itself to a smooth flawless pristine condition. Satisfied, he turned his attention to the large painted logo covering the side.

Larry glanced over his shoulder and shouted, "Now I'll show you how it strips." He flipped a second switch. The shaft holding the padded wheel started spinning at a furious rate. Larry guided the stripper over the logo. The paint disappeared as effortlessly as erasing a pencil written note. With a couple strokes of the shaft, he cleaned off the few bits of residue dripping from the truck. Larry turned off the machine. "Pretty good, huh? What do you think? Want a piece of the action?"

Given their inability to speak, Nino and Dino enjoyed a heightened sense of sound. Hearing a round load into the chamber of a semi-automatic, Nino reached back, withdrew his handgun and rapidly unloaded six slugs into the chest of the man in the black-and-white photograph.

Before the sixth bullet left Nino's gun, Dino un-holstered his .357 and fired. With a single shot, Larry's head exploded, sending the back of his brain into the cleanly stripped side of the truck.

Nino approached his victim. Sprawled face up, the

man they had been hunting bled out into a nearby floor drain. A thick red gunky mix of blood and bodily fluids tinged the large diamond stud in his left ear. The force of the gunshots tore his red toupee from his scalp. Nino pulled out the photo and dropped it on the man's chest. He looked around the garage. The Guatemalans were nowhere in sight.

. . .

It was dusk when the Jeep slowed to a stop a block off Atwells Avenue. Nino reached for the plastic bag. He followed Dino up the sidewalk to the back entrance of Carmen's cheese shop. Pausing, he listened, glanced at Dino and nodded.

Dino charged forward driving his shoulder into the door. He rolled into the back room, drew his weapon and squatted in a firing position.

As Nino quickly dove in behind him, the cheese shop lit up like *WaterFire Providence*. Hot lead rained down in all directions. Just as Nino suspected, the fat sloth planned to finish the job his amateur henchmen failed to execute.

"*DIE YOU COCKSUCKIN' MUTES!* You ain't gonna take this old fuck down!" Carmen unloaded another slew of gunfire.

Nino hugged the ground as bullets whizzed overhead. Waiting for the current round to subside, he realized there was only one way out of this mess. Carmen set them up and now he had to go. But why the double cross? Did the old man think he could find less costly enforcers? Was he worried Nino and Dino wanted a piece of the action? Was Carmen worried the brothers grew tired of being his muscle? After all, when pumping iron, muscles get strained. Nino knew it was pointless to ponder the reasons behind the setup— instead, he rapidly processed his options.

The volley of blazing metal paused. He heard Carmen reload. Nino crawled across the floor behind the cheese vat, stood and fired one round—*BOOM!*— into the back of Carmen's skull. The bloated blimp plunged face first into the water tank. The milky white liquid quickly turned bright red resembling a smooth silky vodka sauce.

Dino reached into the murky emulsion and fished out what was left of the Carmen's head.

Nino grabbed the bag of rotten cheese. Two days of unrefrigerated captivity in smoldering heat had transformed the dairy ball into a putrid mold-covered wad of decay. As Dino held Carmen's head back, Nino forced open his mouth and stuffed the rancid, fungus-infested glob of *formaggio* down his throat.

The Paul Revere Job

Tommy "The Trucker" Dellaventura leaned out the brick tenement's third floor window and laughed. "You call yourself a wiseguy? You ask me, you're a dumb guy. What kinda mobster locks his keys in his own Caddy?"

Al "No Ass" Diageo, cigarette dangling from his mouth, struggled with the wire coat hanger snaked down the driver's side window of his Seventies era Cadillac. "Go fuck yourself, Tommy." Dressed in tight cream slacks and a matching two-tone cardigan, his white pompadoured hair jiggled as he struggled to unlock the door. Exasperated, he paused to catch his breath. Glancing up, he continued his verbal assault. "You're a real *cucksucker*, you know that?"

"Hey, hey, hey. Watch your language, ya filthy old fuck. Ya got little ones runnin' 'round over there." Like most sunny spring afternoons, screaming kids from Saint John's school filled the Polcari playground. "They hear that kinda talk, they might turn out like you. Besides, use proper English. The word is *cocksucker, with an 'O'*."

Al violently yanked the metal hook. With a big grin, he swung open the door. "Ya see that, asshole?" he asked, glaring at Tommy. "Now who's the dumb guy? And as far as my English goes, the word for you is *cucksucker*, with a 'U'. You know why?"

Tommy raised his middle fingers.

"Because you're a *cunt* who sucks *cock. CUCKSUCKER*." Al hopped in the car, flicked his cigarette butt out the window and drove off.

The canary yellow sedan roared up Prince Street and careened onto Hanover, nearly mowing down a crowd of tourists.

Tommy's cell phone vibrated. "The Boss" flashed across the screen.

· · ·

"Michael."

"Tommy. Stick with Tommy, sir," Special Agent,

Michael Bartone said, as he removed his sunglasses. "It helps me stay in character. Less chance of slipping up."

FBI Assistant Director, James Casey invited his undercover asset to take a seat. "I like the look," he said, pointing at Tommy's leather jacket. I'd love to trade my suit and tie in for one of those."

Tommy grinned and ran his hand through his long black hair. "I guess this is what they call business casual."

As the director in charge of the Boston field office, Casey's jurisdiction spanned Massachusetts, Maine, New Hampshire and Rhode Island. Having made a name for himself in New York as the man who brought down John Gotti, the hard-edged lawman was a legend in the Bureau's war against organized crime. Tall and lean with a military style haircut, the veteran agent had never married. Known for guarding his privacy, he avoided office functions, including the annual Christmas party.

Conventional wisdom was that the New England branch of La Cosa Nostra died with the demise of former Providence boss, Raymond L.S. Patriarcha. For decades, Boston's Angiulo Brothers—seven in total— had operated the local chapter out of a small Prince Street apartment building in the city's North End. Gennaro "Jerry" Angiulo, the ringleader, was a certified sociopath. Thanks in part to the duplicitous Irish mobster, Whitey Bulger, the Angiulos succumbed to FBI wiretaps in the early 1980's. With the agency's eventual shift in focus toward combating Islamic terrorism, funding for investigating the American Mafia evaporated.

Casey, however, fought on; he had both the stature to get the right people to listen and the influence to steer budget dollars. Despite the North End's gentrification, Casey felt the neighborhood still harbored a healthy population of Italian street hoods. The kind that likely held the keys to a treasure trove of unsolved crimes. He firmly believed that the old guard seen shuffling along the sidewalks each day, hands clasped behind their backs, knew where the bodies were buried.

"How's it going?" Casey asked.

"As planned," Tommy said. "Got an apartment on Prince. Spend most of my time mingling. But so far, it's what I thought; nothing other than small-time thugs and old-school has-beens."

"Do they trust you?"

"Seem to. I heard they vetted me through their network. Or what's left of it. They bought the story of me being a West Coast based truck high-jacker. These helped." He raised his right foot, showing off his custom-made leather cowboy boots. "Rick Walker's, Newbury Street."

Casey smirked. "Those must blend in nicely with

their track suits and chunky sneakers."

Tommy laughed. "I think these guys keep Adidas and New Balance in business. I have to admit, they are quite an entertaining bunch."

"Be careful. Those bastards might seem harmless, but they're still killers. Don't let your guard down."

Tommy turned serious. "Understood."

"You're sure they bought the backstory?"

"The history we planted about me running over an LA gang member with a hot load out of LAX seemed to excite them. I told them I relocated to the Northeast hoping to avoid retribution from the guy's brother."

"Did they ask how you plan to earn a living out here?"

Tommy nodded. "Told them I'm trying to commandeer trailers out of Logan."

"And no issue with the age difference?"

Tommy shook his head. "Said I was forty. Figured the weight I gained from eating pasta every day bought me ten years."

"Yeah, but you probably still look anorexic compared to most of them."

"True. Al, the guy I aligned myself with, is a bit of a stick, but the rest have the other kind of eating disorder."

"Walking heart attacks?"

"Mmm, hmm. Diabetes, hypertension, prostates the size of melons, you name it. Practically every health issue known to mankind and their proud of it."

"Well, just make sure you don't stand out like a sore thumb."

"No, it's all good. I think some of them see me as the son they never had. Took me under their wings like they're gonna show me the ropes."

"Sound like great mentors," Casey said dryly. He slowly revolved in his chair and gazed out the tall window. His 20th floor Government Center office provided a bird's-eye view of the North End. "These guys have been at this game for a real long time."

"Sir," Tommy hesitated, questioning whether to offer his initial read of the situation. "I know you have strong feelings about this case, but—."

"It's early." Casey spun back around. "I've seen this before. What looks fruitless on the surface can eventually reveal a cadre of finds."

Tommy nodded.

"New England has its share of major unsolved crimes—both murders and robberies. Do I need to list them?"

Tommy shook his head. "No need. I've done my homework."

"Good. Tell me about the goon you've aligned yourself with. What'd you say his name was?"

"Diageo, Al. He's the youngest—a little over sixty, divorced, no kids, chain-smoker. They call him "No-Ass".

Casey smirked. "Pancake?"

"Took a bullet to his backside in his younger days. Tried to avoid the hospital by pulling out the slug himself. Three days later, half of his ass looked like a human cannonball. Gangrene. Doctors had to cut off his right glute. Walks a little gimpy."

Casey grimaced. "What's his racket?"

"Small time crook. Con man. At least he was. Lately he's living off Social Security like the rest of them."

"How'd you meet him?"

"The local café. Wiseguys' version of a coffee klatch."

Casey nodded. "Was probably an up and comer in the Angiulo days."

"They're all gone, right?"

"Correct. Frank, aka 'Frankie the Cat', was the last one. The accountant. Died a few years ago; heart failure. Connolly personally brought him in back in eighty-three."

John Joseph Connolly Jr. was someone all new recruits learned about in training, but avoided discussing around the office. The former FBI agent was sentenced to 40 years in Florida State Prison at Raiford for conspiring with Bulger and his Winter Hill Gang to rub out a known associate. Tommy had heard Casey worked side by side with the dirty cop so was careful to avoid the subject around his boss. The mention of his name caught him by surprise. "Yeah, so like I said,

I just started pumping this guy."

"What are you getting out of him?"

Tommy shrugged. "Nothing, yet. Trying to make inroads with him. Been harassing him to earn his respect."

"Makes sense. That's how those assholes think. Talk their language and they'll sing. Next thing you know they start bragging. They can't help themselves. Lead us right to the pot of gold. I've seen it time and time again. They're all the same. Uneducated hoodlums. Okay, good work."

Tommy took the signal that the briefing was over. "Thank you, sir."

Casey showed him out. "I'll be in Washington for a few days. I'll check in with you when I'm back."

• • •

Wedged between two drab, four floor walk-ups, halfway down Endicott Street, stood a heavy black iron gate. Always locked, it guarded a short dark alley which led to the entrance of the North End Drum and Bugle Corp. Officially the headquarters for the Italian street festival marching band, the social club also served as the unofficial base of operations for local rank and file mobsters. A select few were provided a key. Tommy slid his into the brass lock.

The odor of burnt meat and clouds of acrid smoke

permeated the air as Tommy eased open the green metal door and stepped inside. He peered through the haze. As expected, the regulars were sitting around the large table in the center of the room eating dinner and playing cards.

He glanced to the left. Wearing a grease-stained apron, Ernie "One Ear" Egidio stood at the small gas stove frying steaks in a cast-iron skillet. A Korean War vet, he turned in his rifle for a chef's hat when an enemy hand grenade left him deaf on his right side. Since leaving the service, Ernie had cooked in nearly every restaurant in the North End. After he developed a pus pocket in his good ear, the board of health, despite each member being offered a generous bribe, forced him to retire.

"Hey, Tommy, take a seat," Jimmy Ito said, tossing his cards down. "You can play my hand. I gotta shit." The heavy-set bookie lit up the room with his powder blue Puma tank top tucked into a billowing pair of matching track pants, cinched tight just below his chest, inexplicitly, by a Gucci belt. Wearing his hair like a sumo wrestler, the pointy-nosed numbers runner glided toward the small bathroom in a pair of crisp, chunky Air Monarch IV's. The gleaming white sneakers anchored him to the ground with cushioned comfort and ease while supporting his bulging feet and twisted arches ridden with arthritis and perhaps the clap.

"Grandson tells me now-a-days the kids say, 'I gotta drop a deuce,'" Wally Scapini said. He reached both hands forward and raked in the cash from the last pot. "Gotta lay off those garbanzo beans, Jimmy."

Wally, a squirrely looking guy, peddled pills to the homeless junkies that wandered the blocks neighboring TD Garden. His dyed jet-black hair, parted down the middle, matched his thick onyx horn-rimmed glasses. The lone crew member with facial hair, he groomed his mustache toothbrush style—in the tradition of Adolf Hitler. Regardless of the weather, he always wore a red nylon windbreaker accented with green and white racing stripes. A gift from a former lover, he'd instructed his wife to bury him in it.

Lying face up, below a black velvet portrait of Sophia Loren and a faded poster of the 1982 Italian World Cup Championship Team, Bruno "The Banker" Bellagio was enjoying his nightly massage. Nude, except for the small hand towel covering his groin, the former loan shark flicked his toes as his masseur, Gus "The Greek" Gemelli, worked his hairy thighs.

The Mediterranean massage therapist wore a wide-collared red silk shirt unbuttoned down to his navel, skintight white double hook-and-bar closure slacks and pink Croc clogs. An enormous gold Jesus medallion rested atop a ballooning bulbous mound of wiry salt and pepper chest hair.

In their heyday, Gus and his late twin brother, Gino, shepherded a stable of young, but legal, girls around in their 1971 Golden Anniversary Continental Town Car offering in-room hot oil rubs at some of the city's finest hotels. After his brother died of complications from syphilis, Gus was too distraught to carry on the business. He came out of the closet and entered private practice. Sliding his hands inside Bruno's legs, he glanced up at the TV above the bar which was tuned to live harness racing from the Meadowlands.

"Hey," Bruno barked, in his deep baritone voice. "Keep an eye on what you're doin', will ya? Don't need ya crashin' inta my ballsack."

"Relax," Gus said. "I can smell when I'm gettin' too close."

"Pitch a tent so he knows where to stop," Wally said.

"I'll pop my rod so your wife knows where to stop," Bruno growled.

"Who ya kiddin'," Wally said. "Ya been flaccid for the last thirty years."

"C'mon on now, boys," Sal said. "Play nice."

Tommy rolled his eyes, draped his jacket over Jimmy's chair and sat down. He glanced across the table and smiled. "Hey, Al. How's the Caddy?"

Al scowled. "Yeah, yeah. Don't break my balls, Tommy." He took a drag on his cigarette and tossed a twenty into the pot.

"Tommy, steak?" Ernie asked from the kitchen.

"Sure, kinda hungry."

To Tommy's right sat Henry O'Donnell, the one Irishmen in the group. Half Italian, the former head of Teamsters Local 25 only qualified for honorary membership under the maternal heritage exemption rule. Having just turned eighty-two, the one-time labor boss retained a full head of fiery red hair.

To Al's right, chewing an unlit cigar, sat Bosco "Old Man" Burrata, last of the Burrata Pizzeria brothers. The restaurant, sold years ago to a national chain, was long known as Boston's heroin headquarters. Wearing a billowing black blouse, given his immense girth, the bald, rotund ex-pizza maker spread his double-wide ass across two chairs.

Sal "Short Thumbs" Salerno occupied the spot to Tommy's left. As the crew's most senior member, Sal was the unofficial boss of the North End. However, unlike traditional Dons, given the group's lack of relevance, he did not command the same degree of respect. While he might not have acted the part, he certainly dressed it—polyester broad collared, short-sleeve, buttoned shirt, neatly tucked into high-waisted white linen pants, held in place by a matching wide vinyl belt. His enormous feet were stuffed into shiny vanilla patent leather loafers topped with gold chain accents.

Prior to his ascent to the throne of the neighborhood

gang, Sal was known as Boston's prince of porn. The old pervert got his start peddling black-and-white 8mm home movies from the trunk of his El Dorado and parlayed his profits into owning all the strip joints that once lined the infamous Combat Zone.

A hefty man, he shaved the hair on his head short, in a horseshoe pattern, and his pubes even shorter. A thumbcuffs-themed BDSM session gone awry accounted for his physical deformity. A true deviant, Sal sustained himself on a regular diet of little blue pills and morning peeping sessions at the windows of the neighborhood Pilates studio. As students filed out the door after class, he greeted each one with a twisted smile while picking his genitals through his baggy trousers.

Grinning from ear to ear, Ernie slid a plated T-Bone in front of Tommy. "Still sizzlin'," he said.

"Thanks, buddy."

Bosco leaned forward examining Tommy's steak. He looked up at Ernie. "You didn't drop any of that pus onto it, did ya?"

Ernie frowned. "You're disgustin', you know that?" He shook his head and headed back into the kitchen.

"I'm disgustin'?" Bosco asked. "I ain't the one oozin' white shit out my ear."

"It's the heat," Wally said. "Slavin' over that stove melts the bacteria inside the pustule. Builds up pressure.

Like steam. He's gotta get it out. Kinda like a boil. Don't worry, Tommy, I see him wipe it on his apron when he cooks. Bosco, leave the po' bastard alone, otherwise we're gonna starve to death."

Henry dropped two cards down and motioned for more. "How's the clammin', Wally? You still raking the flats down in Rhode Island?"

Wally nodded. "Me and the wife head down in the truck camper every weekend. Can't get enough a those clams. How're the fish runnin?"

"Not bad. Been trollin' the waters south of Quincy lately. Less polluted."

"Here ya go, Henry," Tommy said, as he tossed him his cards. "What about you, Al?"

"I'm fine."

"Uh, oh," Henry said. "Al's got a winner. I'm out."

Bosco threw down a card. "He's fulla shit. Bluffin' like always. C'mon, Tommy, hit me."

"I'll take a couple," Sal said.

Tommy dealt one to Bosco and two to Sal.

Sal gently rubbed his stubby thumbs over the plastic-coated paper as if he was attempting to stimulate them.

"Put your money where your mouth is, ya old fuck," Bosco growled. He tossed a fifty in the pot.

Sal laughed. "Bosco's right. Al's always bluffin'. A natural born con artist. Just like when he told us he threw out his back. Bullshit story so he didn't have to help carry the statue for the feast. Lazy bitch."

"Bullshit my ass," Al said. "Had to piss in a bottle it was so bad. Couldn't walk. Thought I was paralyzed." He hacked a typical smoker's cough across the table and tapped his cigarette ashes to the floor.

"Lazy in the legs," Bosco said. "Ever since you was a kid. That's what we used to call you."

"That's his ass," Wally said. "He walks funny cause he only got half an ass."

Al raised his middle finger.

"Tommy's got a bad back, don't ya, Tommy?" Henry asked.

"Used to," Tommy said. He dropped a few cards on the table and took three new ones.

"All that weight liftin', I bet," Henry said. "Used to watch those Africans down in Walpole pump iron out in the yard all day. Not for me. Healthy livin' no good for ya."

"Tommy does yogurt," Sal said. "Ain't that right, Tommy?"

"Yoga," Tommy said, correcting him.

Bosco grinned. "Thought that was for fags?"

"I heard that," Gus shouted from across the room.

Wally giggled. "Maybe that's why Tommy wears those boots. Lotsa cowboys are queer. I sawr a movie once."

"Fags my ass," Sal said. "Tommy's not stupid, are ya Tommy? Young guy like you. I've seen those broads going into that Indian temple above the bank. They wear pants so tight you can see their privates."

"It's a Yoga studio, Sal," Tommy said, "And show some respect."

Sal frowned.

"You're done," Gus said, finishing Bruno's massage. He took a seat at the bar and turned his attention back to the horses.

The lanky shylock climbed off the table and flopped his pasty naked body down on the brown leather sofa against the wall. He reached his hands high above his head, kicked out his legs spread eagle and yawned. "Could fall asleep right here."

"Fo' Chrissake," Al said, shielding his eyes with his hand. "Put some fuckin' clothes on, will ya? I'm gonna have nightmares."

"This is for you, Al." Bruno lifted his right butt cheek and blasted a sharp clapping cloud of flatus out his exposed anus.

Al grimaced.

"Minus the shit mist," Sal said, "the unclothed human body is a beautiful thing. Ya got nuttin' to be ashamed of, Bruno."

"I call," Tommy said. He tossed three twenties into the pile of cash and showed his hand—three aces and two kings.

Al slammed his cards down. "Your pot," he growled.

Bosco leaned back and howled. "I knew you was bluffin'."

Tommy reached for his winnings.

"Ernie," Al, snapped, "bring me some a that vino you made last week."

"Comin' right up. Anybody else?"

"Nah," Bosco said. "Tastes like vinegar."

"No thanks," Henry said. "Just took my meds."

"How 'bout that," Al said, "Irishman passin' on a drink."

"Go fuck yourself, Al," Henry said.

Ernie popped the cork out from a large glass jug, filled a red plastic cup and brought it over.

"Sal's right about those chicks," Wally chuckled. "I was behind one of 'em the other day. She was wearin' those skintight pants. Michelangelo couldn't have sculpted a finer ass."

"Those girls are all college graduates," Tommy said. "Not like the *boutons*, those whores, you scumbags chase around."

"What's wrong with whores?" Sal asked.

"I'm warnin' ya, Sal," Tommy said. "One more word and I'm gonna make those thumbs even shorter."

Sal raised his eyebrows.

"Tommy's right," Bosco said. He rammed his finger into his ear and dug out a chunk of wax. "Shut the fuck up. Them are nice girls. And you guys do chase boutons. They're diseased. I know." He flicked the dark gunky glob of waste across the room.

Al chuckled. He blew out a plume of smoke and took a sip of wine.

"What you laughing at?" Bosco asked.

Al slapped his thigh. "Nuttin'. Just thinkin' 'bout Sal's third stag when you was rollin' 'round the floor bare ass with those hookers."

Bosco's round puffy face turned red. "Those were the days."

Tommy pictured the visual, debating if he wanted to throw up or laugh. Remembering Casey's advice, he simply put Al's comment out of his mind.

Sal slammed his small hands down on the table. "*OKAY*! Enough. Let's talk business. Al, you workin' on anythin' new?"

"If I was," he said, motioning toward Tommy, "I wouldn't say it in front a this guy."

"Relax, Al," Tommy said. He set the deck of cards aside. "Don't worry 'bout me. I just like bustin' your balls." He stabbed his fork into a piece of meat and took a bite.

Al grunted.

"I heard ya was schemin' on somethin' to do with the lottery," Bosco said.

"Too complicated." Al tapped his cigarette ash to the floor.

"We'll decide if it's too complicated. Let's go. Spit it out," Sal said.

Defeated, Al threw up his hands. "My cousin, 'Slow Hand' Sammy. Owns a convivence store down in Brockton. We was thinkin' we could rig it so no one ever won the jackpot. He gots one a them machines that makes tickets. All the blacks down there buys 'em. Gets a piece from the state for every one he prints. We figured he'd sell a ton of 'em if none of those degenerates ever won. They'd be lined up for blocks to get 'em." He waved his hands from side to side. "Like I said, too complicated."

Ernie pulled up a chair. "I don't get it. How's you gonna do that? Sounds too complicated."

Al shook his head and sighed. "Ernie. What'd I just say? You listenin'?"

Ernie shrugged. He squeezed his left earlobe and smeared a white blob of discharge on his apron.

Tommy glanced down at his steak. He set his fork down and gently pushed the plate forward.

"Sammy was afraid we'd get pinched," Al said. "State watches that shit real close." Holding his cigarette classic style—between his first two fingers—he pointed at Bosco. "What 'bout you? Got ya hands in anythin'?"

"Matte' a fact, I do. Hear 'bout that fundraiser they got goin' for the Prado?"

"The Paul Revere statue?" Wally asked, scratching his mustache.

Bosco nodded. "And the park behind the Old North Church. They want to fix the bricks and clean the bronze. Polish the granite base it sits on. They call it *restorin'*."

Al's ears perked up. He leaned forward. "Didn't they do that like thirty years ago?"

"Yeah, but they have to do it every so often," Bosco said. "Birds always shittin' on it."

Wally giggled. "They gotta wipe the bird shit off the horseshit."

Bosco frowned.

"*You dumbass*," Sal barked. "Don't be thinkin' a stealin' that money. That's for the good of the neighborhood. You lookin' for easy cash, why don't ya just knock over Mike's Pastry? They ain't connected no more. Like everythin' else 'round here now—*commercialized*. Nice lady walks to the bank every mornin' at seven. She slips me a cannoli every now and then."

Wally smiled. "Sounds like you slipped her your—"

"Uhn, uhn, uhn," Sal interrupted, wagging his finger. "Don't you say it, you perverted fuck."

"That's a good one," Wally said. "A perverted fuck callin' me a perverted fuck."

"Who said anythin' 'bout stealin' the cash?" Bosco asked. "And knockin' off Mike's be like emptyin' the candles in Saint Leonard's. Burn in Hell for that shit. Ya know, Sal, ya might be the big boss but ya think small. That's your problem, ya don't think big. Ya always thinkin' small."

Sal scowled. "Yeah, you think big like the big fat fuck ya are." He puffed out his cheeks and reached his hands out in a wide circle.

"Ya think small, Sal," Bosco continued. "Small like a midget. S—M—A—L—L, small." Squinting, he made the tiny finger gesture holding his thumb and index finger straight and close to each other without touching.

"Little people," Wally said.

Everyone glanced up at the sound of the toilet flushing.

"Dwarfs," Jimmy chimed in, returning from the bathroom. He grabbed an empty chair and sat down.

"Save that PC shit for those liberal assholes in Cambridge," Bosco said. "I stand by what I said. Sal thinks small. And you," he said pointing his cigar at Jimmy, "smells like dogshit in here. You push out your innards?"

Jimmy shrugged. "Wally's right. Fuckin' garbanzo beans. And what are you talkin' 'bout? At least I don't have leaky pipes."

"Gimme a break," Bosco said, "Can't find adult diapers in my size."

"I been eatin' those for years," Henry said. "Wife

puts 'em in soup. Never made anythin' that smells like that. Fuckin' ass smells like seafood. You sure your insides ain't rotten' away? Could be a medical thing."

"Probably that goddam Chink food he eats," Al said.

"Japanese," Jimmy said. "I was raised on that shit."

"Jap, Chinaman, Eskimo, whatever," Al said. "Can't tell the difference. Like those phony monks selling prayer cards. I'd like to stick a gun in their face every time I see 'em hustlin' tourists."

"Thought you was 'fraid a guns?" Jimmy asked. "What kinda mobster doesn't carry a piece?" He patted his ankle. "Got my iron right here."

"The kind that got half his ass shot off and doesn't want to accidently shoot off the other side," Al answered.

"Leave Jimmy alone," Henry said. "He's only half Jap. Ain't that right, Jimmy?"

Jimmy nodded. "My old man knocked up a hooker in WWII. After the war, he set her up with her own massage parlor and then ran off with one of the girls. I took my mother's last name after that. Felt it was the decent thing to do."

"Explains why you became a bookie," Al said. "You people love gamblin'. It's in your blood. All you see at those Injun casinos. Bus 'em in from New York."

Jimmy shook his head in disgust. "You're a goddamn racist, ya know that?"

"I'm a racist?" Al said. "How 'bout you not willin'

to take bets from those ragheads sellin' fruit over at Haymarket every weekend?"

"I thought they were towel heads?" Wally asked.

"Sand niggers," Henry said.

"That's business," Jimmy snapped. "Their credit's no fuckin' good. They're broke. All they do is sell that rotten fruit. No money in that shit. Can't be chasin' 'em when they gotta pay up."

Wally giggled. "You're just afraid they gonna cut off your head."

"*ENOUGH!*" Sal turned toward Bosco. "Finish with your big idea."

Bosco leaned forward and lowered his voice to a whisper. "Bronze. Four tons of bronze." He sat back in his chair. "You know what that's worth?" he asked in a normal volume.

"What'd I say about the neighborhood? You leave that mother fuckin' statue alone, *you stupid bastard,*" Sal said. "You know the tourist money that thing brings in? All those jamokes takin' their picture in front of it after they shovel a bowl of ronies in their face. Keeps the restaurants in business. All those Spics that work in the kitchens givin' us their cash for drugs, whores and bets."

Ernie laughed. "Yeah, the tourists don't even care if the Ricans burn the ronies."

"*Mushade,*" Wally said.

"Mushy pasta is the worst," Henry said. "And I ain't even Italian."

"That statue's worth ten grand," Bosco said. "I got a guy on the North Shore that'll melt it down into bricks. We can sell 'em to Jews. New York, Diamond district, Brooklyn, whateve'. That easy."

"You're outta your mind," Al said. "That's a whole lotta trouble to go through for ten large. Sal's right. That's probably what Mike's drops in the bank every mornin' from a daily cannoli haul. Not even' countin' cookies." He leaned over, stubbed out his cigarette butt on the floor and squashed it with his foot.

Tilting his head toward Bosco, Wally said, "He's a Roman. Not like us Neapolitans. They think they're smarter than us. Got all the ideas."

Bosco folded his lips inward, jerked his head and flipped his palms over. "I said my peace. You got a bette' idea, speak up."

Tommy glanced around the table seeing if there were any takers.

Sal scanned the room stroking his chin. "I'll just say this." He gazed up at the ceiling.

"Don't worry 'bout it," Ernie said. "Checked for bugs last week. We can speak freely here."

"All I'm gonna say, is years ago…" He paused.

"C'mon, will ya?" Ernie barked. "I'm an old fuck. Not sure how many minutes I got left."

"Years ago," Sal continued, "I heard there was this big job and the real money is *under* that fuckin' horse." He folded his arms across his chest and narrowed his eyes.

"The only thing below that horse is the granite it sits on. Worthless." Bosco said. He waved his hands forward dismissively. "You buy that shit at Home Depot these days."

Sal shook his head. "You geniuses figure it out. That's all I'm gonna say."

Ernie raised his eyebrows.

Al sprang from his chair. "I'll see you jackasses later."

Tommy locked eyes on the hotheaded scam artist as he burst out the door.

. . .

Casey's growing frustration was obvious based on the long moments of silence. AirPods in his ears, Tommy stared at his phone waiting for his boss to respond. Pacing along the Greenway at the height of lunch hour, he glanced around ensuring nobody was eavesdropping.

"I'm not buying it," Casey finally said.

"Sir–"

"I simply can't believe that all these guys are talking about is rolling the local pastry shop and a harebrained scheme to melt down a city landmark. You've got to come up with something better than that, Tommy."

"There really isn't much else going on. All I've seen is small-time gambling, minor drug sales and a few over the hill prostitutes. These clowns spend most of their time clamming, fishing and playing with themselves. We're talking about the last of the old timers and trust me, they're aging fast."

"That's the point. There's a history there and you have to find it before it's too late. These buffoons can unlock the mysteries we've been trying to solve for years. Trust me, Tommy, this assignment will make your career."

Or break it, Tommy thought. "I have to be honest, sir. These guys aren't exactly the front line. I mean, I wouldn't even call them the back-up team."

"Let's talk in a week."

. . .

Tommy spun the chair around and sat down, draping his forearms over the top rail. Most mornings, the regulars gathered outside the Café Sporto by eight to sip espresso and admire the young college girls who passed by. Tommy checked his watch. He had thirty minutes before the others arrived.

Al hypnotically stared across Hanover Street at the large bronze statue of Paul Revere. Holding his cigarette twee style between his thumb and index finger, he took a drag and blew out a long stream of smoke into morning traffic. Maintaining his gaze, he asked, "What the fuck you lookin' at?"

"You, you miserable prick. You really oughta give that up, ya know. Not healthy."

"Fuck healthy. Been smokin' these since I was six. Keeps me alive." He made a fist, raised it to his mouth and coughed.

"Don't say I didn't warn ya."

"I won't"

"Where'd ya run off to the other night. You have a date, or somethin'?"

Al turned. "Yeah, somethin' like that," he said with a deadpan look.

Tommy nodded toward the Prado. "Don't tell me you're actually thinkin' about that crazy scheme Bosco came up with?"

Al raised one eyebrow. "Might not be so crazy?" He reached down, grabbed his coffee and took a sip.

"Okay, let me get this straight. First, ya gotta figure out how to hoist the most recognizable four tons of metal in the city out of one of the most tourist filled neighborhoods without being seen. Then, ya need someone with the means to melt it down and make bricks out of it that's gonna keep quiet. And lastly, ya need to find somebody to fork over the cash. That statue is a work of art. Museum kinda art. This is big time stuff. Not so easy. Good luck."

Al glanced around. "Ya know, Tommy, I know a lot about art theft. Wouldn't be the first time I pulled off that kinda heist."

Tommy smirked. "C'mon, Al. Don't throw that bullshit at me. I look like a jackass?"

"Ya want me to answer that?"

"Okay, let's not start talkin' shit again."

"Suit yourself." Al took another puff. "Ya gonna get a coffee or ya just gonna sit there and break my cubes all day?"

"Nah," Tommy said, patting his stomach. "Had the shits this mornin'."

"That's too bad. Consider yourself lucky."

"They got medication for that kinda thing now, ya know?"

"Fuck that shit. I take enough goddamn pills."

"So, what kinda art jobs ya done?"

Al flicked his butt into the gutter. He sat up straight, puffed out his chest and squinted. "There been a few. Gems, doubloons, tapestries, that kinda thing."

"See, What'd I say. You're fulla shit. Climbin' through the window of one of these walkups and making off with some old lady's costume jewelry, Susan B. Anthony coins and area rugs ain't what I call art theft."

"Well, ya hear what Sal said about where the real value is in that statue?"

"Mm-hmm."

"I heard those things too. Years ago."

"I assumed he meant the granite it sits on. And like Bosco said, that's worthless."

Al glanced around again. He lowered his voice. "It's what's inside the base," he said, in a hushed tone.

Tommy leaned back from the front of the chair and rested his hands on his thighs. "Al. You're killin' me. Enough with the hidden treasure pirate mystery. Spit it out, already."

"Look. All I know, is when I was makin' my bones—'round thirty years ago, before my divorce—I got wind of a big job. The whole street was talkin' 'bout it. I was a young soldier tryn' to make my mark. Got lucky and was assigned a small part in it. Was s'posed to help transport some loot. I was just the driver. Some other guy was gonna broker the goods. Didn't know what, where or when. Wasn't sure if it was a new job, an old one or just movin' shit 'round to keep people from findin' it—cops, Feds, other wiseguys. Told to wait for a call. Maybe gotta head to New York, Philly, Providence—no idea. The call never came. Captain on the job didn't tell me the whole story or how all the pieces fit together. That's how they did things then. You're only given a little part. That way there, ya can't blow the whistle on anybody or get pinched."

"That's how it works, huh?" Tommy flashed a mocking grin.

"Don't patronize me, smart-ass. Ya wanna hear my story, or don't ya?" Al snapped. "Might learn a thing or two," he said smugly.

Fuckhead. Just give me one thing I can use to put you away for life, Tommy thought, you ignorant halfwit asshole. "Yeah, I do, actually," he said feigning as much sincerity as he could muster. "But wait. What kinda money ya talkin' when ya say a big job? Thousands?"

Al shook his head. "Like when ya call a guy a millionaire. He ain't just got one. Not two. He got millions."

"G'on."

"Like Bosco said, they was restorin' the statue at the time of this other big job I was involved in. They took the statue away to clean it and left the pedestal it sits on all open on top. They had plywood around it so water couldn't get in and fuck up the granite. Well, things started gettin' crazy 'round here back then. Our kind killin' each other, heat from the law, people fightin' for power. Just nuts. No one trusted no one."

"So, what happened?"

"The guys runnin' the job needed a place to hide the stash. Rumor was, they buried it under the statue. Horse goes back on after they clean it and the loot is safe. They figured once things settled down, they'd use one of their bricklayer buddies to get it."

"So, what makes you think it's still there?"

"That's why I ran off the other night. Drove up to an old age home on the North Shore. Guy I know up there also was workin' on a piece of the job like me. But like I said, we didn't know how the pieces—"

"Yeah, Yeah, Yeah. I got it. No whistle blowin' and all that shit."

"Or pinched."

Tommy rolled his eyes. "Right, whatever. So, who's the guy?"

"Ain't important. What is, is he was the bricklayer. Said he didn't get to do his part. Never heard back from the guys who hired him. Figured they died off, got locked up for life, maybe sent to the chair; who the fuck knows."

"So, what'd your buddy end up doin'?"

"Had to put food on the table, ya know? Moved to Peabody and built chimneys. Poor bastard developed arthritis. Hands all crooked and shit. Walks like a hunchback. Not a cripple or anythin', just a little crooked, that's all. Made a good livin' though, until he got old timers."

Tommy tilted his head with a quizzical look. "What the fuck is old timers? Ya mean he's in a nursing home?"

"Not just old. Ya know, when ya don't remember shit. Like people and that kinda stuff."

"*Alzheimer's*. You mean Alzheimer's, you dumb

fuck." Tommy shook his head in disgust.

"Whateve'. Ya know what I mean. Don't matter what ya call it. What matters, is that tells me the stash is still under there."

"I don't know, Al. Ya said yourself he don't remember stuff. How ya know he remembers this thing right?"

"He remembers. Trust me."

Tommy thought for a moment. "So, what's your game? Go in with Bosco and tell him what ya told me or wait 'til he lifts the horse and then grab the real money?"

"Bosco's a jackass. I know how to handle him. Small timer. Worse than Sal. I'm in it for the long haul. Be set for life. Maybe move to Florida. Get outta this rat-infested neighborhood with all these yuppies." Al directed his gaze at a cute young blonde walking past. He started at her legs and slowly worked his way up to her face. "Then again, maybe it's not so bad 'round here."

"Okay, what's next?"

"Look, Tommy. I think I said all I'm gonna say. Ya want me to go on, I think we gotta talk business. Ya know, negotiate."

Tommy nodded. "Okay, let's negotiate."

• • •

Before risking another potentially embarrassing conversation with his boss, Tommy set out to vet Al's story. He knew just where to start.

When Ernie wasn't making love to his cast-iron skillet, he could usually be found in the club's basement making wine. Festive Italian folk tunes blared from below as Tommy descended the old rickety wood stairs. *"Need help stomping?"* he shouted over the deafening noise.

"Hey, Tommy, how you doin'?" Ernie asked. Pants rolled up to his knees, he stood barefoot in a half oak barrel full of mashed grapes. Sweat poured through his white tank top and dripped from his hairy shins into the vat of dark must. He turned down the music. "Sorry 'bout that. My ear," he said, pointing to his right lobe. "Thanks, for the offer, but I just finished." He carefully climbed out of the sea of juice.

"Thought they banned that kinda thing, with the feet that is? Nowadays, don't they use machines?"

"Not if ya wanna do it right. Grapes ferment better with foot fungus." He grabbed his left ear. "Mix in a little pus too. Natural bacteria. Only way to make wine. My grandfather learned me."

"I'll have to remember that."

"Whatya doin' here so early? Card game don't start for three more hours."

"Wanted to drop these off." Tommy handed over a butcher wrapped package of steaks. "Buddy a mine owed me a favor. Thought ya could put them to good use."

Ernie smiled from ear to ear. "Thanks, Tommy.

That's awful nice a ya. Trust me, I'll fry these babies up nice and black. C'mon, let's put 'em in the fridge."

Tommy followed him upstairs.

"While I got the icebox open, how 'bout a cold one?"

"Yeah, sure."

Ernie grabbed two beers and sat down at the bar.

"Quite a conversation the other night, huh?" Tommy asked, pulling up a stool.

"Bosco's scheme?"

"Yeah. Wasn't sure who's angle was more bizarre. Bosco for thinkin' it up or Sal's mystery about what's underneath it." Tommy took a swig.

"Well, we all got our tales to spin. Been around as long as we have and ya see lotsa shit." Ernie tipped back his bottle.

"What d'ya think?"

"Years ago, was workin' in a restaurant on Fleet Street. One night, right b'fore closin', couple cops, or so I thought, waltzed through the kitchen. Turns out they had just finished dinner in the back room with a connected guy and didn't wanta be seen leavin' out front."

"How ya know who they was eatin' with?"

Ernie flashed a serious look. "Only connected guys get to use the back room."

"Got it."

"Anyhow, they was in a hurry. Like they was runnin'

late. Few months pass, we start hearin' stories like Sal was talkin' 'bout."

"That's it?"

"That's it. Ya don't ax a lotta questions in our business. Know what I mean?"

Tommy nodded.

"So, to answer your first question, 'bout what I think. Who the fuck knows. At my age, don't matte'. I'm happy fryin' up meat and makin' vino. Who knows how long I got left. Bosco wants a melt that horse down, whateve'. Sal thinks there's gold under it, have at it. Just happy I'm still alive."

Tommy grinned. He raised his bottle and tapped Ernie's. "What makes ya think they wasn't real cops?"

"Since we was closin' up, I was doin' the dishes. When they passed by, one was touchin' his face like this." Ernie slowly pressed his index finger into his upper lip.

"What for?"

"Had a mustache. Both of 'em. But not real ones. At least the guy who was pushin' like this." He repeated the movement with his finger. "It musta been fallin' off on account a the hot water I was usin' to clean the dishes. Steam melts glue, ya know."

"I didn't know that," Tommy said, acting impressed.

Ernie raised his right hand. "Swear on my grandfather's grave. That's how we used to open up mail when we wanted to steal checks. Then we'd close the envelope back up and send it off like nuttin' ever happened. Anyway, I think they was wearin' disguises."

"Ya think?"

Ernie nodded and took another drink. "They was only pretendin' to be cops. Ya know what that tells me?"

"What?"

"They was headin' to a big job."

"Ya think?"

"I think."

"Hm." Somewhat amused at Ernie's afternoon entertainment, Tommy nonetheless found the tales he was spinning informative. Unsure if there was any connection with what he heard from Al, he listened on.

"Like that movin' picture story they made here few years ago 'bout robbin' Fenway. They dressed up like patrolmen and robbed the Red Sox. Pretty good idea. Wish we'd thought that. At least I got to be in the movie."

"You acted in the film?"

"Yeah," Ernie said, beaming. "Paid me fifty bucks to walk down the sidewalk."

"Good deal. Let me ask ya this. Ya think Al mighta been mixed up in that job?"

Ernie shrugged. "Who knows. That was a long time ago. I can't remember if I shit yesterday. That's why I eat a prune every mornin'. Figure I'm safe that way."

"Makes sense."

"As far as Al goes, be careful with that asshole. He's a two-faced liar. Wouldn't believe anythin' that prick says. Double crossin' cancer stick suckin' con man."

Tommy grinned. "Don't hold back."

"Well, that's all I know, Tommy. Been 'round a long time, but not long enough to know for sure if there's anythin' buried under that fuckin' horse."

"There's still time, Ernie. Maybe we'll both find out one a these days."

Ernie smiled. "I do remember one other thing ya might wanna check on."

"What's that?"

"Gus said somethin' once 'bout one a his clients. Queer guy owned one a those art places over on Newbury. Gus use to rub him so good, the fairy would doze off. Next thing ya know, the homo's talkin' in his sleep. Sayin' shit like the mob double crossed him on some big job. Buncha nonsense. Might have somethin' to do with what Sal was talkin' 'bout."

"Maybe."

Ernie laughed. "Look at me playin' detective. I'da made a good cop, no?"

Tommy smiled.

"Not too late to turn rat, right?"

Tommy patted Ernie on the back. "Thanks for the beer, buddy."

"No, thank you, Tommy. Appreciate the company and I'll save one a those steaks for ya. Be sure to swing by later."

. . .

"Fuckin' Ernie. Sharp as one a those blades he uses to slice those sides a meat he fries up," Gus said. "Yeah, I remember the guy. Haven't seen him in years. Disappeared overnight just like that. Heard he moved out west." He yanked the sheets off the massage table and tossed them in the hamper.

Gus's small studio reeked of musk. The one room spa, tucked away in an old storefront on Salem Street, resembled a Roman bath minus the sacred pool. The walls were covered with frescos of naked men and the ceiling was painted sky blue with a splash of puffy white clouds. A bronze oil rain lamp erotically lit the dark space.

"What happened to Venus?" Tommy asked, pointing to a statue of the nude male Greek god, Eros, glowing under the lubricated strands of fishing line.

"Swapped her out. More appropriate. And the fragrance helps the guys who can't take the pills on account a their heart conditions."

Tommy nodded. "So, tell me more, about the dude who skipped town."

"Art dealer. Had a gallery in Back Bay. Place in

Rhode Island, too. Newport, Providence, somewhere down there. Moved hot goods for a fee but was more a playah than anythin'. Liked to act like he dealt in serious shit, but I knew he was a sham. Like your goombah, Al. Fuckin' smokestack stinkin' ash heap." Gus grabbed a new fitted sheet from the cabinet.

"How'd you meet him?"

"Probably knew a guy who knew a guy. Ya know how that works. Don't mind me askin', Tommy, why ya so curious?"

"Just wonderin' if Bosco and Sal are on to somethin'. Lookin' to get in on a score, that's all. Not sure if it's worth my time."

Gus nodded. "I get it. Don't blame ya. Those two talk a lotta shit, but they haven't earned their keep in years."

"You miss the old days?"

Gus smiled. "Don't I ever. Miss my brother. The girls. You name it. Things just ain't the same no more. Neighborhood. Business. There's one thing I don't miss, though."

"What's that?"

"Havin' to hide who I was." Gus bowed his head.

"Hey," Tommy said. "Fuck that shit, right? Ya are who ya are. Don't need to worry 'bout that kinda thing no more, no?"

Gus smiled and wiped away a tear. "Thanks,

Tommy. I really appreciate that."

"Don't mention it."

"Ya sure ya don't want a massage? On the house."

Tommy raised his hand. "Nah, I'm good. I'll take a rain check. Thanks anyway."

Gus nodded. "So what else can I tell ya."

"Ernie said somethin' 'bout him talkin' trash 'bout the mob and what they owed him?"

"Yeah, that sounds familiar. Guy was an odd duck. Would fall asleep when I rubbed him. I didn't mind. Saved me from havin' to service him." Gus winked. "When he woke up, I'd just tell him he did real good and he bought it."

"Nice."

"Anyhow, this one time, he starts babblin' about he was gonna move the stash from a big job to some rich Europeans. Said he was promised a cut. Had the buyer all lined up, then everythin' went silent. Never heard from anybody no more. Freak woke up and that was it."

"He didn't say what the loot was?"

"Uh-uh. Like I said he peddled paintin's but cheap crap. Kinda shit you see at Walmart. He'd pull the tags off and mark it up a hundred times. Told me he'd go over to Chinatown, buy some ceramics and claim it was antique Asian art. His big thing was coins. Would go down to Mexico and buy this fake pirate gold and claim it was recovered treasure from old shipwrecks. Dumb ass rich bluebloods be forkin' over cash left and right. Serve 'em right. That's assumin' what I heard was true. All I know, this nutcase coulda been dreamin' when he was sleep talkin'. I was just happy I didn't have to get him off. Had godawful hygiene. Stank like the back of a garbage truck in August. Nasty thing."

Tommy grimaced.

"Now that I think of it, I remember hearin' the guy was in debt up to his ears. Broke son of a bitch. Only one guy at the time puttin' money out to lowlifes like that."

"Bruno?"

Gus nodded. "Might be worth your time to see if he knows anythin'."

"I'll do that."

Gus checked his watch.

"I'll let ya go."

"Don't mean to rush ya, Tommy, but I got an appointment soon and these guys don't like bein' seen comin' in here, if you know what I mean?"

"No worries. I get it. Thanks a lot, Gus. I'll see ya 'round." Tommy headed out the door.

"And don't forget that rain check," Gus called out.

. . .

"Love it up here," Bruno said, reaching into the bird cage. "Get away from all the shit in this world."

The five-story building's rooftop deck provided a

360-degree panorama of the city.

"Beautiful," Tommy said, admiring the scene. Even better than Casey's view, he thought.

The retired loan shark slowly moved between coops, meticulously measuring the correct amount of seed based on the number of pigeons in each. "Not like the movies; my line of work, that is. Most people think I used to bring clients up here when they couldn't pay and dangle 'em off the roof."

Tommy glanced down at the street. "I can understand that."

"Well, maybe a few. But no, I ran a legitimate business."

"C'mon?"

"Tommy, look at me." Bruno jabbed his finger into his face just below his right eye. "Do I look like I would lie?"

"That some sort of trick question?"

"No trick. Trust me. I ain't like Al. Now, he's a liar. All the family members I had that died a cancer and that cigarette suckin' black lung is still alive. Then people wonder why I don't go to church. Ain't right."

"Life's funny like that, no?"

"Who the fuck knows. Anyway, I ran an honest business. Most people think I got my start by holdin' up a bank." He wagged his finger. "Uh-uh. I was no different than all those bluebloods. Family money."

"Gotta love it, right?"

"That's right. You understand. Take this piece of real estate. My father bought it before the war. Between the rents from the restaurants and the apartments above 'em, the place is worth millions. When my old man passed, I took out a thirty-year mortgage at five percent and put that money to work at ten. Made a killin'. They call it 'Leverage'. No different than those wasp bastards on Wall Street."

"No different."

"Here." Bruno handed over the bucket of seed. "Wanna feed 'em? It's peaceful. Makes ya calm. Try it. They won't bite."

"Thanks, Bruno."

"Make sure ya count first. More than three birds, I usually go with a couple pinches. Like this." He squeezed his index finger and thumb about an inch apart.

Tommy peered into the next cage. Seeing four feathered creatures he spread his fingers and reached into the mix. Prior to releasing the food, he glanced over his shoulder ensuring his teacher approved.

"The Guinea small businessman gets a bad rap in this country," Bruno said, vigilantly chaperoning his pupil. "Like me, for instance. Cunt judge accused me once of rapin' borrowers on interest rates. The term is, 'Usurious'. Bullshit. Told the bitch I make an honest margin no different than any other legitimate bank.

Got a nephew who works a stand-up job at State Street. Not mixed up in our thing. Told me to use the words, '*Risk Reward*.'"

"What'd she say?"

"She axed me if I actually knew what that meant. Told her I found the question to be an insult. Gave her the *Bras d'honneur*."

"The what?"

"Ya know, the Italian gesture—the umbrella salute." Bruno extended his left arm in a slightly bent heil Hitler and grabbed his bicep with his right hand while slightly jerking his head toward the sky. "Go fuck yourself. She got the message."

"Bet she did."

"My people got no choice. Can't go to a real bank. Bad credit, don't pay taxes, ya know how that kinda thing works. And if they run into trouble, I'm a reasonable guy. I work somethin' out. I'm willin' to negotiate. Take a few more points, some fees, extend the term. As a last resort I might have to break a few bones. Got no choice. Hey, I wanna get paid, right?"

"Right."

"Not like those white-shoe banker fuckheads. Those cocksuckers 'ill pull the rug right out from under these poor people if they can't pay their mortgage. Colored, Spic, Chink, don't matte'. Fair lendin', my ass. They take the house, throw 'em out on the street and get what eve' they can get for the place. No difference if it's a mansion or a shithouse. Rat's nest or a palace. Not me. I negotiate. Ya doin' good, Tommy. You calm?"

"I'm calm."

"So, Gus said you needed some help with somethin'"

"Yeah, doin' some diggin' on that scheme Bosco was talkin' 'bout. Tryin' to see if I should go in on it."

"Good to do your homework. You're a smart kid, Tommy. And Gus is a good guy. Even bein' a fruit and all. Gotta give him credit. Gives a good rub no matte' if you do or don't want his special endin'. And let me be clear, Tommy, I don't. Not my thing, ya know? I like the women. All my life."

Tommy nodded. "No doubt. Me too."

"And I said it before, but I'll say it again. Watch out for that jerkoff, Al. Wouldn't trust that shitbag for anythin'. Devious scoundrel."

"I heard that."

"For what it's worth, my advice is watch him like a hawk. Ours is a rough industry. Ya know, Tommy, it's always the ones you trust that fuck ya. I learned that a long time ago."

"Thanks, Bruno. How'm I doin'? Doin' okay?"

"Doin' fine. You calm?

"I'm calm."

"See how happy those fuckin' birds are? Anyway, Gus said you asked about the guy with the art business?"

"Yeah, he thought he might've been in hock with you."

Bruno shook his head. "Nah. That piece a shit was a dope head. Owed Wally some serious scratch. Came to me askin' if I'd bail him out but I didn't want any part of that shit. I always required collateral. All he had to put up was some shitty trinkets and worthless pictures. Told him to fuck off."

"Good to know."

"Yup, the number one thing that brings people down is drugs. Never fails. Don't got mixed up with that shit. Didn't want any part of it. Wally's got his thing, but not for me. Stay outta drugs, Tommy. Stick with the clean stuff: robbery, hookers, gamblin', shylockin' blackmail. Nuttin' wrong with makin' an honest livin'. Trust me, ya won't regret it."

"Thanks, Bruno. Appreciate the advice. I'll check with Wally 'bout that guy." Tommy finished the last birdcage.

Bruno patted him on the back. "Ya did good, kid. You calm?"

"I'm calm."

. . .

"Always do the most business in front of 7-Eleven." Wearing his trademark windbreaker over white track pants, accented with red and green side stripes, Wally waved to some of his regulars. Like sedated zombies, the herd of toothless unkempt junkies meandered aimlessly in front of the convivence store. "C'mon, let's duck down here. Walk 'n' talk."

Tommy followed the sleazy pill dealer around the corner.

Hands clasped behind his back, Wally glanced up at a modern apartment building. "Fuckin' real estate racket eatin' up my territory. Drivin' all the homeless garbage out to Sommerville."

"Sorry to hear that."

"*SON OF A BITCH*." Eyes bulging, Wally stopped, lifted his right foot and stared at the sole of his large white sneaker. "Fuckin' feces." He scraped his shoe against the curb, frantically trying to rid it of the putrid smelling excrement. "Not like it used to be 'round here. Wouldn't find fecal matter back in the day. See that construction project," he said, pointing to a high-rise steel skeleton. "The derelict who pinched that loaf used to be able to go into that empty lot to shit. Now they gotta defecate right on the sidewalk. Goddamn crime. Why I don't pay taxes. Ain't right."

"Fuckin' government. Can't trust 'em."

"No shit, huh? They're all on the take. Corrupt bastards. Let these fuckin' Russians in. Commie bastards nearly put me outta business." Wally scratched his small moustache.

"How so?"

"Ya think I been pushin' pills to these vagrants my whole life? Fuckin' opioid addicts. Uh-uh. Used to deal in the good stuff: coke, crack, meth, PCP. That's where the real money is."

"Serious business?"

"Oh, yeah. Ya know, I was like CVS. I bought from distributors and I was the retailer. No different. Guy in Providence supplied the powder and candy and I got the rest from an old fuck in Connecticut."

Tommy decided to hedge his bets. If Al's story turned out to be a wild goose chase, maybe he could offer Casey a drug distribution ring. "They still in business?"

"Nah, just like up here. Things turned sour years ago."

Tommy's heart sank. "Too bad."

"Tell me 'bout it. We all took a hit. Well maybe not Al. Remember what they say, Tommy; can't con a con man."

"I'll remember that."

"Yup, ain't like it used to be. My thing was no different than Jimmy's business. Redman does a war dance in Washington, next thing ya know, they're called a tribe and get to build casinos. Where the fuck was their tribe a hundred years ago?"

Tommy shrugged.

"I'll tell ya where. Nowhere. There was no tribe. Ya know why?"

Tommy shook his head.

"'Cause they ain't Injuns. They don't look like Injuns, they don't sound like Injuns and they don't dress like Injuns. Look at me. I look I-talian, I sound I-talian and I dress like an I-talian. Drunkard savages."

"Things ain't so bad, no?"

"Henry's the only guy who came out on top. Crazy Irishman's got a Teamster pension. What'd I give for one a those babies. Wouldn't have to hawk this junk." Wally pulled out a bottle of pills from his pocket and shook it.

"Not easy, Huh?"

"Not at all, my friend. Anyway, gettin' back to what you axed me before. There's only two guys I can think a back then that owed me serious coin. Now ya gotta remember, Tommy, that was a long time ago. My memory ain't that great, ya know what I mean?"

Tommy nodded.

"One of 'em, I think the guy Gus knew, completely vanished. I heard the other one moved up north; Maine, New Hampshire. Out in the woods like some kinda animal—real hillbilly. No surprise bein' a druggie and all. Music kid I think. Went to that school over by the Pru."

"Berklee?"

"Right, not the one in Californi. Worked at some museum in town."

"Ya remember which one?"

"No clue. But there's somethin' else that sticks out in my mind." Wally tapped his index finger to his head. "My wholesaler from Connecticut got wind I had a couple bums who were extended. Wanted their names."

"Did ya gave him the names?"

"I gave him the names. Didn't want no trouble with the guy—real crazy fucker—and didn't want him to cut me off. I was makin' a good salary back then, ya know what I mean?"

Tommy nodded. "So, what happened?"

"Next thing I know, he sends me an envelope. Tells me it's to cover the tabs for the two schlubs. I don't ask no questions, just happy to get my money. As far as those two went, I never sawr 'em again. For the best. Couple a losers."

"Whatd'ya figure happened?"

"My guess is they had somethin' my guy needed. Maybe they could help him with a score. He musta made a deal with 'em. They call that a *quid pro quo*."

"That what they call it?" Tommy acted impressed.

Wally nodded. "Latin. Nuns taught me that when I was a little shit. Those Cat-licks learn ya real good. So, like I say, they took care a him, and he took care a their bills. That's how this business works."

"And that's it?"

"That's it."

Tommy paused.

"No, wait," Wally said. "Now that I think a it, 'round that same time, my source in Providence was lookin' for help too. Needed to stash a big payday. Had to hide some serious loot before he went away. Our kind do that all the time, ya know? Then when we get outta the can, we dig it up. Kinda like Social Security, right? Wiseguy version of a retirement fund. Don't know how he made out 'cause he ended up in the big house for a while."

As they neared the next block, Henry and Jimmy rounded the corner. Both men appeared upset. They approached with stern looks across their faces.

Wally stopped and turned toward Tommy. "Looks like we reached the end of the road."

. . .

After six hours of digging, Tommy needed a break. He glanced up from his laptop; at just past midnight, he rubbed his eyes, refilled his coffee and paced the small apartment. The Bureau's sophisticated algorithms had narrowed the population, but still hadn't identified a clear-cut link between past crimes and what—if anything—was entombed under Paul Revere and his horse, Brown Beauty. Tommy mulled over the list:

Crime:	The Great Brink's Robbery
Date:	January 17, 1950
Location:	600 Commercial St. (@ Prince St.), Boston, MA
Value:	$2.8 million ($30 million today)
Suspects:	Apprehended and convicted
Property:	Only $58,000 recovered
Assessment:	While event date precedes time frame, Al's "Big Job" might have been a subsequent heist of the remaining original haul.

Crime:	The Great Plymouth Mail Truck Robbery
Date:	August 14, 1962
Location:	Route 3, Plymouth, MA
Value:	$1.5 million ($13 million today)
Suspects:	John "Irish Red" Kelly–Acquitted
Property:	Never recovered
Assessment:	Vincent "Fat Vinnie" Teresa (Died 1990) claimed to have laundered the proceeds on behalf of Kelly. Al's "Big Job" might have been a subsequent movement of the laundered funds.

Crime:	The Bonded Vault Heist
Date:	August 14, 1975
Location:	101 Cranston St., Providence, RI
Value:	$30 million in Cash, Gold, Silver and Gems ($143 million today)

Suspects:	Numerous—Mastermind, Raymond L. S. Patriarca
Property:	Never recovered
Assessment:	Al's "Big Job" might have been moving the stolen goods after Patriarca's successor, Raymond Patriarca Jr. was indicted for racketeering, extortion, narcotics, gambling and murder on March 26, 1990.
Crime:	Isabella Stewart Gardner Museum Theft
Date:	March 18, 1990
Location:	25 Evans Way, Boston, MA
Value:	$500 million + ($10 million reward)
Suspects:	Numerous organized crime figures
Property:	Never recovered
Assessment:	Facts surrounding the heist appear to fit Al's storyline—however, level of sophistication and ability to execute such a crime is well beyond his and known associate's abilities.

Tommy let out a long sigh, dropped to the floor and pressed out fifty push-ups. Exhausted, he fell into bed.

• • •

"You think he's going to stab you in the back?" Special Agent, Bill Curtis asked. The curly-haired techy ran surveillance for the Boston field office from inside a white windowless van labeled, *Blue Harbor Clams*.

"Don't know," Tommy said. He stared at the small video monitor. "What I do know, is if this operation goes down in flames, my next assignment will be delivering mail at headquarters."

"Well, let's see." Curtis slipped on his headset. "looks like it's show time."

Cigarette dangling from his mouth, Al crossed Christopher Columbus Park and headed toward the Rose Kennedy Garden. Bosco sat waiting on a bench just behind the long trellis that overlooked the harbor. It was a dreary gray day along the waterfront. A light drizzle rhythmically pinged the roof of the van.

"Got your message. You wanted to talk?" Bosco asked. He opened a large black umbrella.

Curtis adjusted the laser microphone.

"'Bout what you said the other night. At the card game. The statue," Al said.

Bosco laughed. "You think I'm crazy too? You ran out like your good ass cheek was on fire. Assumed you were annoyed or somethin'."

He waved his hands from side to side. "No, no. Only annoyed I didn't think of it first."

Bosco puffed up his chest and pursed his lips.

"Wow," Curtis said, "this guy's good."

"Yeah," Tommy said, "I told you he's a con artist. Plus, Bosco loves to have shit blown up his enormous ass. Al ain't gonna double cross me. I still think he knows more than he told me about what's entombed under that statue. The key is if he keeps quiet about it with Bosco." Both men turned their attention back to the screen.

"I think I can help; for a piece, that is." Al took a drag and blew out a cloud of smoke into the rain.

"What makes you think I need help? And how big a piece?"

"Gotta a buddy with a crane. Twenty-five percent."

"I gotta truck, and no more than twenty." Bosco extended his free hand.

Al shook. "I'll be in touch."

Bosco nodded.

Al pulled his jacket over his head and headed toward Hanover Street.

Curtis removed his headset. "Looks like we're in business."

• • •

Tommy exited the surface level Green Line train at Coolidge Corner. Glancing up at the S.S. Pierce clock tower, he realized he was late. With the operation at a critical stage, he didn't want to risk being seen entering Government Center. He arranged an in-person with Casey at a nearby hamburger joint.

"You want to grab something?" his boss asked, already halfway through his lunch.

"No, I'm good." Tommy pulled up a chair.

"Curtis filled me in on the recon mission and I read your email summarizing your conclusions. Nice work. Here's my question; you really think those bozos are serious?"

"They're dead serious."

"And you're convinced the real payday is under that horse?" Casey took a bite of his burger.

"I think Al knows more than he's letting on. My guess is maybe they held up a bank back in the day. Might've buried the cash inside the base of the statue. Cash, gold bars, gems, who knows. Whatever it is, he's adamant it's worth millions."

"And you believe him?"

"Yeah, I do. As I laid out in my note, I tried to vet his story; but look, it's a gamble. As you saw, when you boil it down, there's only a handful of large-scale crimes that fit the bill. But over the years, there were many smaller bank holdups that aren't as well known. It could be anything in-between."

"But you have no idea what SPECIFICALLY might be under there?"

Tommy shook his head. "I combed through all the obvious cold case files and didn't find any reference to the statue as a possible hiding place for the stolen goods."

Casey sipped his milkshake.

Tommy wagged his finger to make a point, then hesitated.

"Go ahead, spit it out."

"Al said something I found a bit odd, even more so after hearing Gus' story."

"Odd, how? Who's Gus?"

"Odd coming from such a moron. You don't want to know."

"Life has its quirks. What did he say? You're right, I don't." Casey removed the lid from his shake and scooped up a chunk of his frozen drink with his straw.

"That he knew a lot about art theft."

Casey nearly spit out his ice cream. "You can't be serious?"

"Serious that he said it, but not like I believe him."

"Everything you've told me about this crew is that they're a bunch of clowns. Excuse me, amateurs."

Tommy nodded. "Yeah, I called him on it. He sounded full of shit."

Casey replaced the top of his cup and drifted in thought. "And what if he isn't?" Before Tommy could answer, his boss sat back in his chair and looked him straight in the eye. "You do realize how that comment resonates related to Boston's most famous unsolved crime?"

"I do."

"Not just any art theft, but the most famous *unsolved* art theft in history."

Tommy saw Casey's enthusiasm begin to build.

While happy his boss's skepticism was fading, he was careful to level set expectations. "Look, sir. The Gardner heist, as well as a few other local high-profile incidents where the property was never recovered, obviously popped up on the radar screen: Brinks, the Plymouth Mail Truck, the Providence Bond Vault."

"Those go back a ways."

"True, but I picked up some intel that the goods might have been moved again years later. Mainly the Providence crime. It sounded like Patriarca Jr. was looking for a place to hide things right before he went to prison."

"I'm more intrigued by the potential connection to the Gardner case."

"My gut tells me there's something under that horse. But I'm not sure I'd put money on it being the missing paintings."

"That story the cook told you about the phony patrolmen sounds awfully familiar, assuming he remembers it correctly."

"That might have been nothing more than a couple of dirty beat cops back in the day picking up their envelopes. As far as the fake mustache theory, the guy might've been trying to hide his face. And if they were wiseguys, goons have been playing dress up like that forever. Look at Brinks, Plymouth and a host of other stickups."

Casey raised his eyebrows absorbing Tommy's argument. "Well, I'll cede this much. I've encountered plenty of hustlers over the years pretending to have access to the stolen artwork only to find out they were bluffing. Most of them were trying to swindle rich black-market buyers or trade for a get out of jail card."

"These guys just aren't that sophisticated. Cash, yeah, jewels, probably, but priceless masterpieces, I doubt it."

"You think that's a bet that dopey bookie in their group would take?"

Tommy weighed Casey's comment.

"Don't answer that. Let's get back to the details. How is this thing going down?"

"It's pretty straight forward. Al thinks I've got an in with the construction union. I told him I can get a crane. That's what he offered Bosco. I'll take a stroll through the neighborhood each night after midnight. The tourists should be gone by then. Al will leave two aircraft warning lights on at the top of the crane. When he hears Bosco has the truck, he'll turn one off. That will be the signal that it's a go."

Casey smirked. "Clever."

"I assume things are all set with the city?"

"Yeah. I arranged for a phony building permit. The crane will be on site tomorrow. And what about the rest of the crew? Are they in on it?"

"Nah. Al cut them out. Typical con man that he is, he told Sal that the rumor about the hidden stash was a hoax and convinced him to let Bosco steal the horse. The only thing Sal expects is for those guys to kick him a little cash from the bronze."

"So, it will just be the two of you in the Prado after Bosco takes off?"

"Yeah. And you'll handle him, right?"

Casey nodded. "Since the pizza man will be headed to the North Shore with the statue, I'll be waiting just past the Zakim. Can't imagine he'd take the Tobin. Either way, we'll have a bird in the sky. You signal us once Al is secured and you've identified the loot."

"Got it. He won't be a problem. He's afraid of guns. Doesn't even have one."

"What kind of mobster doesn't carry?"

"It's a long story."

"I assume you'll be armed, regardless?"

"Always. But like I said, Al won't be any trouble. Surprised, but no trouble."

"Tommy," Casey said, crumpling up his burger's wrapper. "If there's one thing I can guarantee, there's always a surprise."

. . .

Tommy stepped onto the sidewalk. The click of his wooden boot heels ricocheted off the neighborhood's brick buildings. While fully lit, the basketball court behind Saint Leonard's was empty. He turned left and headed toward Salem Street. Despite being open twenty-four hours, Bova's Bakery was deserted. The night owls had long gotten their fix of late-night calzones and pastries.

Tommy weaved his way through the steep narrow streets surrounding Copp's Hill Burial Ground. He headed down Charter Street, eventually emerging onto Hanover, just east of Engine Company Eight. Glancing up over the roof of the firehouse, he could just make out the tip of the crane.

. . .

"*This is the truck you got?*" Al threw up his hands in disgust.

"Quiet down, will ya? You'll wake the firemen." Bosco climbed out of the white Ford pickup.

"And could ya pick a brighter color for a night job?" Al said.

"It's my brother-in-law's. Gimme a break. Ya wanna do this thing or what?"

Tommy kneeled down and peered under the frame of the dual wheel truck. "Al's right, Bosco. Ya know the payload capacity of this thing?" Tommy stood up and pointed to the statue. "We drop that in the bed and it might squash this truck like a bug."

Bosco waved his hands back and forth. "You two pussies leave things to me. We tow his boat with this vehicle. Forty-footer. We go for blues. Never had a problem. C'mon, let's go. Al, get your half-ass in that crane so we can get outta here."

Al flicked his cigarette into the dark and climbed into the operator's cab. He fired up the engine and began pushing and pulling the long metal levers. The boom soared wildly over the roof of the neighboring building.

"You sure you know how to work that thing?" Tommy asked.

Al maneuvered the joystick, slowly steadying the arm over the statue. He pushed a button and a pair of metal straps descended, stopping just above the giant horse.

Tommy lifted himself up onto the base and secured the harness under the animal's belly. He jumped off and signaled Al to proceed.

Al shifted the motor into low gear. A deep moaning hum rumbled through the quiet neighborhood. The massive structure jerked away from its pedestal and floated skyward into the darkness. The long boom reached out toward Hanover Street. Al dropped the cargo into the bed. The rear bumper sank to the ground, while the hood rose at a steep angle.

Bosco climbed into the driver's seat. The truck leveled off.

Al climbed down and joined Tommy on the sidewalk.

Bosco leaned over the passenger seat. "I'll be in touch," he said, through the open window. He sat back, turned the ignition and floored the accelerator. The engine roared. The pickup lurched forward in fits and starts before slowly rolling up Hanover Street.

"I'll be right back," Al said. "I wanna make sure he doesn't break down before he gets to the tunnel. Don't want him walkin' back here while we're diggin' 'round."

Tommy eyed Al suspiciously. "Okay. But hurry up. We ain't got all night."

Al broke into a limping trot toward the Greenway.

Tommy surveyed his surroundings. Despite the Prado being filled with vagrants most nights, not a soul was around; it was as if they had been warned to avoid the park that night or perhaps been relocated. Growing impatient, he hoisted himself back up onto the granite base.

The enormous stone slabs formed a hollow oval cavity lined with masonry blocks. He shined his cell phone flashlight into the dark hole. Tommy peered inside. A blue tarp, held in place by two antique looking objects, covered the interior space. Musty air, likely trapped for years, mixed with concrete dust, wafted up.

Tommy honed in on the two artifacts securing the cloak. The larger item appeared to be a cross between a large pedestal candle holder and an ancient trumpet. He was more intrigued by the smaller piece, a bronze eagle. His mind raced. Did he just open a time capsule from the American Revolution? Wait, he thought, the statue wasn't that old. Did someone pull off a heist of historic relics and burry them here? Was any of this connected with the job Al described? There was only one way to find out. Tommy slowly lifted the plastic sheet.

One by one, a pattern of small circles pressed together in a honeycomb pattern appeared. Balancing himself carefully on the edge of the stone wall, Tommy leaned in closer. The circles appeared to be tops of old rolls of wallpaper.

"Jesus Christ," Tommy muttered aloud. If this turned out to be a redux of unsealing Al Capone's vault, his career at the Bureau was toast. Tommy reached down, grabbed a tube and headed over to a bench under one of the park's old-fashioned lamp posts. In better lighting, he realized what he thought was wall covering, was actually rolled up canvas. His heart beat faster. Hearing footsteps, it nearly stopped. He glanced up.

"Speechless? Or should I say, priceless?" Casey stood a few yards away aiming his FBI issued semi-automatic straight at Tommy's head.

Unsure of what was unfolding, Tommy maintained his composure. "Al will be back any minute, sir. I haven't secured him yet. He ran up the street to make sure Bosco made it to the tunnel. I thought the plan was for you to cut him off on the highway. It's just me, sir. You can lower your service weapon."

"I could, but I won't." Casey stepped forward. "Your gun. Throw it in the hole. Real slow."

Tommy reached into his jacket, unholstered his firearm and tossed it into the statue's pedestal.

Casey motioned toward the bench. "What do you have there, Michael?"

Hearing his real name gave Tommy a cause for concern. He gazed down. "I believe it's a painting, sir. There are more."

Casey stepped closer. "Never thought I'd see these again."

Tommy considered making a move but hesitated given he was staring down the barrel of his boss's 45mm. "Were you one of the thieves that night at the Gardner?"

"No. Those were a couple low level goons. The ones your buddy the cook saw. There were rumors flying all over the place about who was in on it. Given the turf wars going on at the time, it didn't take us long to figure out it was the Italians. Bulger was pissed they cut him out of the deal, but he had his own demons to battle. The bottom line was Wally's supplier from Connecticut bought off the security guard, the Berklee kid he mentioned. Made it worth his while. Offered to pay off his drug debt in exchange for access to the museum. Told him if he refused, he'd kill him. It was that simple. The Angiulos were in prison by then, so I used that to my advantage."

"You cut a deal with them?"

"Tried to. They were still calling the shots from behind bars. I offered to facilitate delivery to a European collector, launder the funds and help get their sentences reduced. The get out of jail ticket was a lot sweeter than what Gus' art dealer client could deliver."

"Did they go for it?"

"Never got to the end zone. Everything went to shit. Internal power grabs, wiseguys killing wiseguys, the Indian casinos arrived and the next thing you know, they all started dying. Their whole organization fell apart. I didn't know who was in charge or who could lead me to the paintings. Over the years I searched everywhere from under backyard sheds in Connecticut to abandoned warehouses in Red Hook. The real crime in this was the sheer stupidity of the idiots who pulled it off. They were so ignorant of how valuable these things were. They had no idea what they had. Utterly clueless. Imagine, they were driving around with these masterpieces rolled up in the back of their Cadillacs like they were old newspapers. If it wasn't for their lack of braincells, I could've spent the last three decades sunning myself on a yacht off the coast of Monte Carlo. I've waited thirty years for this day."

"So, have I," Al growled.

Tommy glanced over his shoulder. Al stood in silhouette against the light from the spier of the Old North Church. His stance implied he was armed.

"Who's this asshole?" Al asked.

"FBI," Casey said. "Drop your weapon, if you actually have one."

"Go fuck yourself," Al said.

Tommy rapidly debated who to align himself with. No matter his decision, he knew he was in deep shit. "Al, I think you should listen to him. He's got us clean."

"He ain't got shit."

"Listen, you old fool," Casey said. "Drop the gun or—"

"*OR WHAT*? You bastards fucked me real good. I had a chance to make my mark when I was a young man. Earn my keep. I was gonna help move these things years ago until ya stuck your nose up my ass and cut a deal with the Angiulos." Al stepped forward.

Despite his supposed fear of guns, Al wasn't bluffing. Visibly agitated, his right arm reached out long, pointing a shiny Magnum revolver at Casey. "*I coulda been a real mobster if it wasn't for you, YOU PIECE A SHIT!*"

"Calm down," Casey said. "Drop your weapon or

the cops will find you splayed out in the morning and assume you're just another homeless junkie that was rolled overnight for their fix."

Al chuckled. "FBI, huh? Let me ask you something, mister FBI man. You sons-of-bitches still wear those bulletproof vests under your shirts?"

"Why don't you pull the trigger and find out?" Casey said, in an I dare you tone.

Al lowered his aim and fired. The shot rang through the Prado bouncing off the brick walls.

Casey withered on the ground, both hands clenching his right thigh as blood spewed through the ragged hole in his pants.

Al pointed the barrel of the revolver at the back of Casey's skull.

"*NO!*" Tommy screamed.

Like the daily canon shot from the USS Constitution, a huge blast echoed through the North End.

"*Jesus Christ*, Al. You just killed a federal agent."

Al tucked the massive piece of iron into the back of his waistband. "A *dirty*, federal agent." He kicked Casey's firearm under the bench.

Tommy's face turned ashen. "I thought you were afraid of guns?"

"Don't believe everythin' you hear, Tommy. This is a tough business, we're in."

"What about Bosco? Did he get away?"

"Who knows. I didn't trust you, so I lied about checkin' on him. I circled back around the church to make sure you wasn't settin' a trap. Had my iron stashed under a bush."

Thinking fast, Tommy gambled that Al snuck up behind them before he and Casey acknowledged knowing each other. "How do I know I can trust you? Somebody set a trap." He motioned toward Casey's prone body. "How'd he know this was goin' down?"

Al glanced down at the dead lawman. Menacingly, he slowly raised his gaze. "Why weren't your arms up when this guy was talkin' to ya? He had a gun pointed at ya and you was just standin' there like ya was pals."

"He knew I wasn't armed. He made me throw my gun over there," Tommy said, motioning toward the base, hoping Al would look away.

"What's with all the shootin'?" Out of breath, Bosco appeared on the sidewalk.

Al spun around.

Tommy lunged forward reaching for the back of Al's waist. His youth and strength were no match for the senior street thug.

"What the fuck is goin' on?" Bosco asked.

"Freeze," Tommy said, shifting the gun's aim between the two capos. "FBI."

"I knew I couldn't trust ya," Al sneered.

"*FBI?*" Bosco asked. "What the fuck you talkin'

'bout? FBI hasn't been 'round here for years."

Al dove for Casey's gun.

Tommy fired.

Al's left ass cheek exploded. "*YOU MOTHERFUCKER!*" He grabbed his shredded glute and crumbled to the ground.

"Oh, shit," Bosco said. He covered his head with his hands and shuffled back toward the Greenway.

Given how slowly Bosco was moving, it was an easy shot. Tommy aimed at the back of his large target. Holding his gaze for a moment, he dropped his arm to his side. He didn't have the heart to blow the obese bastard away. Instead, he turned around, sat down on the bench and drove his razor-sharp boot heel into Al's maimed ass.

Al shrieked. "I'm gonna kill you, you *cocksucker*."

"I thought it was *cucksucker*?"

"Go fuck yourself, Tommy," Al growled.

Michael turned his attention back to the canvas he had recovered before Casey ambushed him. He slowly unrolled the painting. As the sun rose over the harbor, he marveled at Rembrandt's only seascape.

Made in the USA
Middletown, DE
24 December 2020